OURSELVES ALONE

&

HOMELESS JACK'S RELIGION

OURSELVES ALONE
&
HOMELESS JACK'S RELIGION

*messages of ennui and meaning
in post-american america*

H. Millard

iUniverse, Inc.
New York   Lincoln   Shanghai

OURSELVES ALONE & HOMELESS JACK'S RELIGION
messages of ennui and meaning in post-american america

All Rights Reserved © 2004 by H. Millard

No part of this book may be reproduced or transmitted in any form or by any means, graphic, electronic, or mechanical, including photocopying, recording, taping, or by any information storage retrieval system, without the written permission of the publisher.

iUniverse, Inc.

For information address:
iUniverse, Inc.
2021 Pine Lake Road, Suite 100
Lincoln, NE 68512
www.iuniverse.com

ISBN: 0-595-32646-3

Printed in the United States of America

CONTENTS

Foreword vii

Part I Ourselves Alone 1
   Homeless Jack 3
   Homeless Jack on Evolution 10
   Homeless Jack And the Subatomic Particles 13
   Homeless Jack on Post-American America 21
   Ourselves Alone 23
   The Great White Fathers And Mothers 25
   Homeless Jack on White Liberation 27
   Homeless Jack on Individualism 33
   Homeless Jack on Chinese Zulus 37
   The New Censorship 41
   Repression of Non-Jews 44
   The New Plantationism 47
   Workers of the Nation Unite! 50
   We're All the Same? 52
   Intolerance, Bigotry And Hatred 54
   Betty Crocker Gets Blended 58
   Eloi And Morlocks? 62
   Ending Bigotry And Injustice 66
   Immigration As Genocide 68

The Madman 70
Disappearing Peoples 73
Is It Racism Or Consciousness? 76
Reclaiming "Their" Heritage 79
Brainwashing of European-Americans 82
Mellow Yellow 85
Another Swastika, Another Religion 88
Life's Losers? 91
Whacko Blenders Push Genocide 94
Can You Find the Hate Crimes? 98
Ugly Duckling Or Swan? 100
Conform! No Pink Monkeys Allowed 103
Not Quite Yourself Anymore, Mon? 106
Unity 108
Homeless Jack Talks Racism And Religion 111

Part II Homeless Jack's Religion 115
Homeless Jack on The Guide 117
The Guide 121

FOREWORD

Some of this stuff in here is by or about me. Some of it ain't. Some of it may sound like fiction. Some of it may not. Lots of it is about stuff that most people don't want to write about 'cause we live in repressive Dark Age times where truth takes a back seat to other things and where free speech ain't what it used to be. The first part of the book has short pieces about things that set the stage for the second part which is mostly The Guide.

Tom July
a.k.a. Homeless Jack
From under the 4th Street Bridge

PART I

OURSELVES ALONE

Homeless Jack

I was born in a box under a bridge that crosses the cement Los Angeles river near Santa Fe Avenue and Fourth Street on a night when you could hear the coyotes howl from the sewer openings, and cancerous looking possums with babies clinging to their backs rooted through the garbage looking like rats from hell. I swear I can remember the sound of a train rumbling by as soon as I was born. My mother was a crazy white homeless whore who died when I was ten. I don't know who my father was, but since I have white skin, my hair was once blond, and I have blue eyes, I figure he must have been white too. My mother said she didn't know who my father was and it was a miracle that I didn't come out part white, part Mexican, part black, part Korean and who knows what else. My mother didn't know much about genetics. I figure my father was probably a crazy homeless person and a junkie. I might be the result of sex for a cigarette. My non-genetic class pedigree don't much matter to me because what's the difference, really, whether I was born in a mansion or in a box. Life is life. At least I was born, and that's a hell of a lot better than the alternative which is non-being and non-existence. Every day I thank God for being alive. I love life. I can't wait to wake up each day to smell whatever is in the air, to feel the breezes on my skin, to see whatever there is to see and to experience new things. You may not think I have much of a life, but you're wrong. This is as much my planet as it is anyone else's and I live my life as I choose. I figure that whatever good or evil I do in life will come back to me, so I try to do as much good and as little evil as possible.

I might be just a weed growing up through the cracks in a skid row sidewalk and not a pampered bush up in Beverly Hills but, by damn, I'm alive and the life in me is as good and genuine as any other life. My mother, God willing, is now part of the great consciousness. She could have aborted me, but she didn't. That tells me that she was more a woman and more of the life force than all the piss ants who kill their babies who live in big houses and who hang out at the yuppie gyms with their little leg warmers and trendy bottled water.

You probably noted that I said my *non-genetic class pedigree* don't much matter to me. If, from that you assumed that my genetic pedigree does matter to me, you'd be right. It does. It wasn't always so, though. I went through an awakening process that maybe many others have also gone through or will go through and I'll explain this a little further on.

You might imagine from the circumstances of my birth that my perspective on life might be a bit different from someone who was born in a hospital to normal parents and who grew up under more normal circumstances. You might be right. Then again, you might be wrong. I don't really know, because I don't know how others think about things—how they really think about things—I just know how I think about things. And what I think, is that life is great. I can remember growing up with the smell of burning rubber from a tire retreading plant near the train yard. Before I was old enough to run real good, my stroller was a shopping cart that my mother used to carry our most precious belongings in. She didn't dare leave anything unattended down by the river because the black homeless people would steal what we left there. We used to collect cans to pick up some extra cash and we used the shopping cart for that too. Every so often the cops would come and grab the cart from her and tell her that if she took one again, they'd bust her for petty theft. They never did bust her for that, though. I figure there was just too much paperwork involved.

When I got to preschool age, my mother was forced by welfare punks to put me in a skid row school with all the Mexican and black kids. I was one of only two white kids there. I didn't think too much about it until some kids started calling me and the other white kid Nazis and racists for no reason other than that we were white and they weren't. That's probably when the seeds were planted that led to my eventual awakening and led me on the spiritual quest that has consumed me all these years. Before they started calling me names, I wasn't even really aware that these others were others. I thought of us all as just kids. After the name calling, things started changing in my mind. It wasn't hatred of them or anything like that, it was just that I started realizing that while people may be the same economically and socially, they might also be very different genetically.

Don't get me wrong, I get along with everybody and everything and I wouldn't hurt a fly or say harsh things to people just 'cause they're different from me, but even though I'm kind to all living things I know that I ain't a fly and a fly ain't me, and I ain't any type of human other that what I am and other types of humans ain't me. Live and let live. I ain't got a hateful or prejudiced (as that term is usually used) bone in my body.

So, anyway, the name calling in school started me thinking—not all at once—but gradually, about what was really important and essential to being who we are. Are we our economic or social class or are we our genes? Then I started thinking about religion and the meaning of life and all that kind of stuff. More about this later.

Now, the other white kid went the other way. He started acting, dressing and talking black. Years later I found out that he married a black girl and had a black kid. Then he died of a drug overdose. I figure his life was just a big waste and he was a dead end. Anyway, the school would give me free breakfast and lunch, and when school was out it wasn't too far to the cement river. The school got used to me and my ways and I passed from preschool to regular school in the same building.

My mother died one night about 2:00 a.m. after coughing up blood. She had gotten real skinny before dying, and she said that she had AIDS, so I wasn't surprised. I moved her body up on top of the bridge where someone would find it and where no one would connect her with me down below. I propped her us so she was sitting in a dignified manner and then I kissed her on her forehead. She just looked as though she was sleeping. I cried a little, but even then I knew that all that lives, dies. It's just part of the big struggle.

I put one of those Mexican candles that are in glass containers with pictures of some saint or other near her body, along with some flowers. The candle I used had a picture of St. Michael killing a dragon. I boosted the candles and flowers from a place down the street where a Mexican gang banger had been gunned down a few days before and where his friends had put the flowers and candles all around the spot. I figured they wouldn't miss a few flowers and just one of the candles, and if they did, tough, they could kiss my ass. I didn't tell the school that my mother had died, and whenever I needed a note or anything signed, I'd have one of the other homeless people write it or sign it. The school never noticed the different writing styles, or perhaps they did, but just didn't say anything. Some things you just overlook on skid row.

When I was twelve, I decided to go on the road. I had a homeless woman write a note to the school saying that we were moving out of the area and then I had her sign my mother's name to it. I gave the note to my teacher and that was that. Simple. Direct. Effective. I was free. After school that day, I threw some stuff in a back pack and jumped the first train heading toward San Francisco. The trip was uneventful and cold, but it was the start of my new life and a new beginning. When I got into San Francisco, I could see the skyline in the distance and headed for the tall buildings the way an animal will head to a drinking hole. I soon landed in the Tenderloin because I heard that's an area like skid row in L.A. and I know how to get around in those kinds of places. The difference between the Tenderloin and skid row in L.A. was that the Tenderloin was way more tooty fruity than LA, but that didn't bother me much. I live and let live. Don't mess with me and I won't mess with you is the Golden Rule. I hung around in San Francisco for a couple of years, just living and learning about life and seeking answers to existence. I met a runaway girl who I hung around with for a time, but then she got hit by a car and died. Once she was gone, there was nothing to hold me in San Francisco so I hopped back on a train and ended up back in L.A. and that's where I've been living ever since. My birth certificate says my name is Tom John July, but my street name is Homeless Jack. I use both names, and some others, depending on circumstances.

That's about all I'm going to tell you about me, because it don't really matter none. This is about philosophy and religion and living, and a buncha of other stuff, not about me. It happened one night as I was out canning that I came upon this other homeless looking guy who also appeared to be canning. We struck up a conversation of sorts. Come to think of it, he started the conversation and it was almost as though he was seeking me out or was put in my path by the subatomic particles or something, but I didn't think much about it at the time. I was going through a dumpster down by Towne Avenue near where the transsexuals do their thing, when I came across him lyin' on the sidewalk looking all beat up.

"Help me, please," said the guy.

"What's your problem, man?" I asked.

"I'm sick. I haven't eaten anything in days."

"So why don't you do more canning?" I asked.

"I have a problem diving in." That's when I saw that he only had one leg.

"You really hungry or are you just scammin' me?" I asked.

"No. I'm really hungry. Can you please help me? I'm gonna die. I just got into town and I don't know my way around." I looked at the guy and he looked sincere. There was something odd about him, though. His eyes were a peculiar shade of blue and they were clear, not blood shot as I would have expected. "What do they call you?" I asked.

"Arman," was his reply.

"That your street name or your given name?"

"It's just the name that I'm known by."

"Let me see if there's any food in this dumpster," I said as I dove in. There was usually something in this one, because it was near a greasy spoon. I looked around but there was no food fit for humans. Then I spotted a bunch of dirty papers stapled together like a book. The cover was just a piece of white typing paper and it was torn and stained but I could read the hand lettered words "The Guide." The cover also had a buncha ball point pen drawings of connected spirals and things that looked sort of like swastikas, and some other things with lines all sort of interweaved. For some reason, and I don't really know why, when I looked at it I was reminded of misty, deep, dark, ancient forests. I thumbed through the pages and some were handwritten and some were typed. Some pages were easy to read and some weren't. I figured I'd keep it. Just then, I noticed that Arman seemed to be watching my every move, but then I just dismissed that thought and figured he was watching to see if I had come up with any food that I might be holding back. I later decided that he really was watching me closely and that he was testing me. I put the book in my coat and climbed out of the dumpster.

"O.K. look, there was nothing fit to eat in there, but I know a joint that is open now. We'll go over there and I'll buy you something to eat, but you got to pay me back sometime, okay?" He nodded that he would pay me back. I picked him up and put him in the shopping cart on top of the black trash bags I was filling with cans and bottles and we headed over to a dirty little coffee joint in a storefront on 7th Street that sold cheap food all night long. "You guard my cans and I'll be right back," I said, as I left him outside in the cart with my cans and bottles. I went in and got a taco and a coffee. After putting about a half cup of sugar in the coffee I went back outside to the guy. His meal took all the money I had. "Look," I said to him, "I gotta get back to canning, before the trucks pick up all the good stuff, but there's some missions over on the next street that will be opening in a little after dawn, and maybe they can help you some more. I took him out of the cart and put him on the sidewalk. He thanked me and I left. "Don't forget, you gotta pay me back, man," I said as I left, all the while figuring I'd never see him again.

"I will," he said. "Thank's for the food, brother. I won't forget it." I returned to my canning route and pretty much filled up the cart with cans and bottles. Then I headed over to the recycling center on Alameda to get some cash. I turned them in and got $7.50, which was a pretty good take.

Anyway, that gives you an idea about my life and about what led up to me getting the book. Lots of times I just tell people that I found the book in a dumpster, but as you've heard, there's more to it. Most of what happened next is pretty boring so let me just say that I started reading the book and then reading it again and reading it again. It ain't that long. I ran into the guy with no leg a couple of weeks later, and he did pay me back. I had finally guessed that he had put the book in the dumpster for me, or someone like me. I tried to return the book to him, but he told me that it was a gift to me and it would bring me good luck and that I should have the book typed like a real book and that it should be sold to people who were somehow called to buy it like I was called.

"See, that's the way it works," he said. "There are hidden connections in the cosmos, and your Essence, call it your blood, if you want, hears things—whispers from the far places—and your blood is called if you have the right stuff inside you. Then, your blood awakens a little more and you start on the spiral path to discover what has called you. God is the whisperer who called you to this book."

"So, why don't I just give the book to others for free?" I asked.

"Cause that ain't the way it works, man," he said. "Those who can hear the whisper as you heard it will have to make a decision in the struggle. Will they part with some hard earned bucks to buy the book or pass it by? See, they get to make a choice in the struggle with their own free will and they have to put some effort into the struggle to get the book, just like you did. Will they choose right or will they choose wrong? It's a fork in the path of their existence that they face and no one can give them a free ride down the right path."

So, that's how it happened. Because you're reading this, then maybe you heard the whisper. Or, maybe not. I don't know. But, you've got the book that Arman talked about. It's at the end of all these short essays and columns. I really do think I was led to find the book. I don't think it was a coincidence that I ran into this guy. Somehow, I think it has all been planned. There are no coincidences.

Anyway, if you didn't hear the whisper in your blood don't worry about it. Just read it on a different level. There are meanings within meanings like you find in an onion. It's sort of as though all people are kind of like radios and some of us are missin' some of the parts and some others have better workin' parts and some weren't born with the right parts. It's like whatever it is that's callin' us is all around us like radio waves or subatomic particles or waves or vibrations or something and has a link to whatever is inside us if we've got the right parts that can tune into these things. It's like with the right parts we vibrate like tuning forks. And, if we've got the right parts and if we think the right good type of things and if we do the right good type of actions then we may receive the signals, God willing. If you ain't got the right parts, and you gotta be born with 'em, and most people on the planet don't have the right parts, or if you've got the right parts but you don't think the right good type of things or if you don't do the right good type of actions then you don't receive the signals. So, the book—The Guide—helps you understand this stuff and think the right thoughts and do the right things. It can't help you if you don't have the right parts, though. Because, then you won't even get it. Now, don't go gettin' confused. When I say right parts I mean Essence. See, you gotta have the Essence, man. That's the stuff you get from your genes that's the blood that Arman was talkin' about.

Now, don't whine that this doesn't sound fair. If you got an argument about this stuff, then go talk to God, He's the one who set this all up and that's the way He wants it. He doesn't go kowtowing to humans or care about what they think is right 'cause He's the boss and we aren't. He isn't the way you think He is. If you think He don't exist that's probably okay by Him, at least on one level. Just call Him nature. Anyway, He made all the things in existence different and he keeps tinkerin' with 'em and re-engineering living things and everything else in existence and He just keeps shuffling the cards of matter and DNA and everything else. He likes things different, that's why things are different. If you weren't born with Essence that's the way it is. You weren't born full of sap like a tree either, so are you pissed off because a tree has sap and you don't? Be who you are.

Some of the things that follow are columns. Some ain't. There's some stuff in here that may help you understand, and it's easy to read and ain't too pretentious. Some of it is me talkin' about life and other stuff. Some of it ain't. It's all kinda alley spiritual, but don't go gettin' any of that smarmy religious stuff goin' in your head 'cause God don't like that dried up husk, bloodless type of religion. Those things are full of death, and this stuff that I know is full of life. This here stuff is what I believe. It's my religion. I figure my religion is real and all others are false, and I got the damn book to prove it, 'cause Arman had me find it and it says what I know inside. Anyway, read on, and you'll get the idea if you're capable of gettin' the idea; if you know what I mean. And if you don't get it, then you probably don't have the right parts, or if you do have the right parts and you don't get it then you may not have the right beliefs or the right actions and if you follow The Guide, you'll get 'em.

[The Guide is in Part II of this book]

HOMELESS JACK ON EVOLUTION

"I'm telling you man, that guy Darwin had some of it right and some of it wrong. See, he thought that the way new species were developed out of old species was mainly because in order to survive in any particular environment or in any particular niche, individuals of various species that were better adapted to survive in that environment or niche lived to reproduce and they produced more of their kind. The others that weren't as well adapted died off.

"So, if a bunch of, say, black bugs living on white sand were easily seen by birds that ate them, they would be picked off and many wouldn't live to reproduce up to their maximum, but if mutant white bugs were born among them who blended in with the light background and weren't as easily seen by the birds then they would reproduce more like themselves until their genes for whiteness dominated the black genes. Soon, there would simply be more of the white genes and fewer of the black genes and eventually the black genes would die off in this particular location and the black bugs would become extinct on this beach. Then, if these white bugs remained separated and isolated from other populations of black bugs on other white sand, in time they would become a new species unable to mate with black bugs from other areas.

"See, now that's probably right as far as it goes, but I don't think it goes far enough. I figure there are other mechanisms of evolution that cause critters to change. I think we pick up things from the environment—meaning just about everything that is around us or that we experience in some way or another—and that sometimes these things become part of us or change us. There are subatomic particles, waves, rays and all sorts of things like that. Then there are viruses or bits of genetic material floating around us in the air we breathe or the water we drink and bathe in and swim in or whatever—I mean we're in a big soup of discarded DNA and atoms and molecules from animate and inanimate things that we can't see. Look at a sunbeam in your room and you can see that the beam is full of small dust particles. Most of these particles are dandruff or dried skin or other things that contain the DNA of the people who have been in that room. We shed tens of millions of skin cells each day and many of them are floating around in the air that we breathe. Suppose we're in an environment full of people like us? The DNA that is all around us in the soup is like ours. Suppose we're in a room full of people unlike us? The soup is unlike us. Get it? If people unlike us have been in that room, then we're in a soup that contains their DNA. That's not good, man. I think that some to these things can change us. I also think that other things, sounds, sights, weather, clothes we wear, places where we live, even things that we think, and many other things also change us. I figure all living things have something of the chameleon in them, but to greater or lesser degrees and that we change to be like what we're around to sort of become one with the nature of where we live. Look, you've seen pictures of those bugs that look like thorns on the plants they live on or walking sticks that look like twigs of the trees where they live. I don't figure they got that way just be selective breeding. I think they picked up atoms and molecules from their environment that helped them change. I think it's the same with humans.

"I saw this news story this week, man, about how people are smarter when they listen to classical music. Hell, we've all heard that story before, but this article presented something new, it seems to give the science behind this getting smarter stuff. According to this article which was about rats, the proper friggin' music caused a gene expression of BDNF, a neural growth factor, CREB, a learning and memory compound, and synapse I, a synaptic growth protein, in their hippocampus, as compared to control rats who had listened to equivalent amounts of white noise. So, the music—sound—caused changes in the brains of these rats. What's that tell you? It tells you that by controlling sound and presumably other things in our environment that we can cause changes to our brains and also presumably to our bodies. Now, put the Darwin stuff together with this and you see that we need to separate out and live in the right environment with the right things comin' in to us so that we can become more than we are.

"Saying we have to separate out is a big leap from what the article says about music, Jack."

"Yeah, but I make that leap because I've seen this someplace else."

"Where?"

"In that religious book I told you about that I want you to retype for me. It has stuff in there that says the same thing but in different revealed ways. It says that we're supposed to separate out from other peoples and live in places that it says are right for us and which will switch on certain genes and cause other changes that will cause us to change or transform or evolve or mutate or something—I forget—into the next step for us."

"How do we know what is right for us? Maybe we're supposed to live the way we're now living and maybe the multiracialists have it right and that all humans are just supposed to breed together," I said.

"Nonsense. That way leads to having just one big similar mass of humanity and doesn't help evolution. That leads to devolution. People think because it's possible for us to live in certain places and in certain ways because of our inventions—heating systems and air conditioning, for example—that this is right for us. It's not. I figure these things just keep us in something like an infant stage and don't let us mature to be more."

"So who says we're supposed to evolve into something else?"

"The book, man, the book. Look, man, you haven't seen it yet. But when I get it to you, you may understand. It's revealed. It's from the highest power."

"That's what many people say about their own religious books," I replied. "Ultimately, one either has to believe them or not, because none of them have any real proof." \

"Right," said Jack, "and I choose to believe what I choose to believe, and if no one else believes it, that's their business, but I'm tellin' you this book has the answers and tells us how to live."

"Geez, Jack, you live in a box down by the cement river most of the time where the air is full of the smell of burning rubber. Is that how we're supposed to live?"

"Don't be ridiculous. That's my personal choice and as far as I know, my life style has nothing to do with the book other than the fact that I've stripped myself of the conventions of society to be better in tune with the essential me and reality."

"Jack, what kind of crap do you think you're taking in from your environment down by the river? If you believe the book, shouldn't you be trying to find some place where what you take in is better?"

"Look, I never said I'm perfect or that I'm the ideal person or that I live the ideal way or anything like that. I'm just saying that I do my best and live in a way that is comfortable to me and gives me the freedom that I need. You just wait until I let you see the book, man, then you may get it."

Homeless Jack and the Subatomic particles

Homeless Jack, the Prophet of God, blew through town again last week like a crazy whirlwind from out of the far places. He was as skinny as ever and his teeth hadn't gotten any better. His clothes were dirty and his gray hair was scraggly and wild looking. Thankfully, he didn't have any bits of food sticking in his beard. Despite his appearance, or maybe because of it, the sub-atomic particles seemed to be with him in a big way. You could see them circling his head like a fuzzy halo around a street light on a foggy morning. The thought crossed my mind that maybe he had been sleeping in a dumpster someplace where someone had discarded radioactive waste of some type.

"Man, I've been having more revelations," said Jack, speaking in that missing front tooth, slight whistling voice of his. "I was told to tell white people that there's a Savior coming to keep them from extinction, and that we need to prepare the way for him, because his birth isn't going to happen without our help. God alone can save our people, but He won't help if we won't help ourselves. God has told me that we must no longer worship Him in false religions created by men, because that's false worship. And, that pisses Him off. He said that our true religion begins in our genes. That is his where He lives—within us, in fullest glory. He's in our blood. He said look inward to find Him, and forget those fancy churches."

"Why white people, Jack? Shouldn't God be looking out for everyone?" I asked.

"Hell, man, I don't know. The Big Guy just tells me some things, not His whole damn plan. I'm just the friggin' messenger or something.

"I was down by the river and He sent a friggin' Angel to tell me these things. It scared the crap out of me at first. Right out there where the cement stops and the channel begins, this Angel just appeared. He was gigantic. Not fat. Just really, really tall. He stood there in the air all shimmering like and said that the only way to save our people is through right religion. Apparently knowing that I am a born cynic, the Angel told me that because of our inborn human psychology, correct revealed truths are the ONLY way to save white people from extinction. These truths have to be revealed and they have to be true. Then he told me that throughout history it has been religions alone that have transcended more than a few centuries to influence men, and that it was mainly religious leaders who caused various civilizations to change direction. Jesus came and changed the direction of a large part of the world. Mohammed came and changed the direction of a large part of the world. Others also did similar things. Get it? It wasn't politics or politicians. It wasn't the big shots of society. It wasn't the rich selfish ones. It was the outcasts who believed that they were hearing messages from God who changed human destiny. Of course, all those guys in the past were wrong—at least as people now interpret them—and I'm right, but that's another story. What white people have lacked is one who has come forth to change their thinking to the right path. Instead of a Savior and a true religion from God, they have been content to follow the religions of others. In the case of Christianity, many white people have wrongly believed that it is their religion. It isn't. It is not a religion of light and life and it is not from their blood. The Big Guy is all about life, man. He'd probably be hanging out at topless bars if he were in human form. He's not with the smarmy types with their phony reverential church voices. They're dead or dying. They have no life. They're afraid of life, because they're afraid of sex. Hell, the Big Guy made sex fun so we'd replicate. Any religion that opposes that is screwy and neurotic. I figure God is about transformation. He wants to transform lower matter and energies into higher matter and energies and he does it with us through sex. Blind evolution can take us in any number of directions, but now that we have big brains we have to take over and direct and will our evolution in the right direction. The Savior may even now be among the eggs and sperm of white people. I believe that there may have been other Saviors who were aborted or who were never born because some white people chose not to have children and died childless, useless lives. They were dead ends. I was told that each white person is to have as many children as possible to increase the odds that the Savior will be born and so that the white kind will cover the universe

"We," said dirty, skinny, missing a tooth, Homeless Jack, "are the next evolutionary step for mankind. Every egg and every sperm should lead to a new white life, because we need vast numbers. I was told that whites need to get out of false death religions that keep down their birthrates and which teach that the flesh is bad and that all people are the same. I was told that white males are to start taking multiple wives in order to increase their offspring. I was told that whites have to be bold in asserting their peoplehood. I was told that they are to organize and to build a white sub-culture within the larger anti-white and non-white cultures of this planet until they can separate out. I was told that whites are to have their own exclusive institutions and their own exclusive organizations separate from the "diverse" institutions and organizations sanctioned by anti-white genocidal governments and evil men. I was told that whites are to separate out from non-whites in every way possible and to live in all white communities when possible, and to keep their distance from non-whites when this is not possible. When whites are unable to completely physically separate themselves from others, they are to join together and build centers of their new religion in the communities in which they live until such time as they can separate. And each believer is to teach others the truth to make them into believers. If there are too few of them in an area who believe, they are to build personal Temples in their homes bearing sacred symbols that they may gaze upon. If they do not have the space for room sized personal Temples, they are to build Temple boxes. If they do not have room for Temple boxes, it is good and sufficient to rely upon sacred symbols that are with them at all times.

"It is time for a new faith. It is time for a new, enlightened, and aware people growing from the rotting corpses of the old white people who are so brainwashed that they are smiling as their extinction looms. It is time for a new consciousness based on the truth that the most important thing we can do to survive is to increase our birthrate. It is time to reject those who say things such as 'I've decided not to have children.' Such people are self-indulgent, purposeless dead ends. It is time to reject those among us who enable our genocide by saying things such as 'Don't put a hyphen in my name, I'm just an American,' or who are holding us back from being what we, by nature, truly are—a distinct people. It is time to separate ourselves from whites who preach our destruction through mixing. It is time for genetic self-determination. It is time for a new species of man grown out of the old via separation.

Whites are alone on this brown planet whether some of them understand this or not. Whites will not survive on the good intentions of others, but on their own struggle to survive. Existence is a struggle and one must love the struggle."

"What does that mean?" I asked.

"Just what it says. If you're unhappy about having to struggle, you don't get it. There is an eternal struggle between being and non-being, between light and dark. The struggle is going on everywhere at all times. It happens on a cosmic scale and on a sub-atomic scale. Good is being and light. Evil is non-being and dark.

"Jack, are you starting a new religion?" I asked.

Call it a religion if you want or call it whatever you want to call it. It is the right way. And, it's not me who is starting it. I'm just a messenger or conduit.

These things, and more, came to me from revelations and they are the will of that which I guess we can call God, but that term may not give the true picture. Let no man, nor governments of men, challenge it. I'm going to live my life according to these things because I believe they really are from God." "And, what if people just say you're nuts?" I asked.

"I expect that. I also expect persecution. It doesn't bother me. Nothing really bothers me since I've seen the truth. It's all part of the struggle. The struggle is eternal."

"Why you, Jack?"

"I don't know. It may be that one does have to be crazy to be able to tune into these revelations. I've got a theory about this, but it's just a theory. I think the force that we call God, or some aspect of God, is all around us all the time, sort of like radio waves, but that one has to have all the right parts and be able to tune into the right frequency to get the revelations. Sometimes I can even see them. For some reason, that I don't fully understand, I have the right parts and am tuning into the right frequency and things are coming in as clearly as though I had just tuned into a powerful radio station. Since others may not be able to tune in, it's my job to tell them what I'm receiving. I call this thing or things—these right parts—Essence. Only our people have this type of Essence. It is born into us, so long as we are born pure. I think it is activated by right belief and right action. The less pure we are, the weaker is the Essence. I've also discovered that I can't tune in if non-whites are close by. Their physical presence seems to block or scramble the waves, or whatever they are." "Maybe it's sort of like you're picking up something from the sub-atomic particles," I offered, as a way to humor him.

"Yeah, maybe. Anyway, for whatever reason, I receive these things."

"Geez, Jack, about half the schizophrenics walking the streets would probably say the same thing. Haven't you heard that most religions are trying to eliminate things from their teachings that cause humans to not like each other?"

"This is different. I can't really explain it, but it's not the same as schizophrenia, and I know many people who are schizophrenics out on the streets. Then again, how does that old saying go? Isn't it something like, "Who God touches, he first makes insane? And, besides, God ain't no pansy. Do you think He's going to conform to what a bunch of humans are doing to screw up what He wants? Hell, He's the big guy in the sky. He's the boss. What He wants and what a bunch of humans want in order to satisfy their own wishes ain't necessarily the same."

"So, how is anyone to know who is, and who isn't, sane, and who has the truth?"

"I don't know. It ain't my job to make everyone believe. I'm just supposed to tell what I was told to tell. I guess people will just have to believe. Faith is powerful. If they've got the right blood, the right belief, and the right actions, they'll know. And, if they keep the symbols with them all the time and look upon them often, they'll believe, and they'll have the right frequency."

"What are you actually doing about the revelations?" I asked.

"I'm looking for a bunch of wives, spreading the word and the symbols, and I'm trying to keep the dark forces from killing me. And, God willing, I will survive. Or, God willing, I won't survive."

"Kill you? Why would anyone want to kill you? You're starting to sound paranoid, now."

"My revelations have the power to completely change the world. They're a new departure. The evildoers have been trying to stop white people from hearing the truth. You know, in some countries people get arrested if they display a swastika or even salute in a certain way or read the wrong book. You know why? It's because these things have the power to revitalize white people and get them back on the right path away from evil and moving toward the light again. The right symbols and right words are religiously powerful. Some of the symbols that are banned, are religious symbols. Banning the type of swastika revealed to me is like banning symbols of other religions. It can't be allowed. Believers must have this symbol. It helps open the Essence and helps them tune in."

"Jack, now you're sounding like you have delusions of grandeur as well as being paranoid and schizophrenic. Look, the business with the swastika and the rest was just to make sure Nazism is stamped out. We all know that."

"No we don't. That's what they want you to believe. The universe is a strange place. There are ancient forces of good and light behind what you think of as a purely political and social ideology and symbols. It's a magical universe…well, actually, our physics just hasn't figured it out yet. The forces of evil and darkness know that symbols and words have power, so they don't want people to use them or even to see them. They're after me to shut me up. Here, look at this." Jack then held out his hand. He was wearing a silver signet ring bearing a sort of rounded swastika with what looked like flames around it. "This is a powerful symbol," said Jack. "Even looking at it can transform some people who have the right genes so that they reject the dark and accept the light. It's the engine of creation and destruction. It is a circle on its way to becoming. It is the Cornucopia of God. It sucks everything in and reshuffles matter and sends it back out."

As I looked at the ring, the room suddenly seemed to be full of tiny particles shooting around and through everything like millions of tiny tracer bullets. There were trails of light everywhere. They crisscrossed in every direction and went through everything as though there was nothing solid in the room. I put my hand out and I could see thousands of these particles pass through it. The mostly empty room was actually alive with, and full of these particles. In a way, the trails looked like thread weaving everything together. About three feet above Jack's ring a bunch of these particles seemed to start swirling around and looked like a spiral galaxy…or a rounded arm swastika or a miniature tornado or hurricane. It was as though this image had been projected up from the ring, or perhaps the particles were captured by the ring and made to form this image. I don't really know. Maybe it was just a trick of my mind, but it was as though I was actually seeing the subatomic particles.

You see them, don't you?" asked Jack with a slight smile. "Now who's schizophrenic? God is making you as crazy as I am so you can see. Look, man, I gotta tell you the truth. I ain't really the messenger. I get this stuff from a book I found in a dumpster, that I figure was put there by this guy with one leg named Arman."

I hardly heard what Jack was saying because I was busy concentrating on closing my eyes to see if I could make whatever was going on, stop. When I opened my eyes, everything was back to normal. For a moment I wondered if Jack had somehow slipped drugs into my coffee.

Just then, there was a knock on the door. "Hide me," said Jack.

"What…? There's no place to hide here. Crawl out the basement window and disappear." Jack did so, and I opened the door and there were two black guys there in suits who looked like feds and who identified themselves as such.

"Can we come in and talk to you?" asked the shorter of the two in that forceful command tone of voice used by cops to make you think that it isn't really a question and that you have no choice but to agree.

I was just about to let them in, when something seemed to snap inside of me. This was my home, my separate place, my external personal…Temple…yes, that's what it was…my home was now my Temple. I did not want it defiled. "No. You can't come in. What do you want?" I asked

"Have you seen this man?" he said, as he held out an old dirty photo of someone who could have been Jack, but maybe not. It looked as though it was from a high school yearbook. Being a law abiding citizen, I was about to tell them that Jack had just left. But then an inner voice told me that I was on Jack's side and these guys weren't on our side and could never be. They weren't part of our people.

"Hmmm. I don't think I recognize that person." I said. "What'd he do?"

"He's a racist."

"Right. What did he DO?" I asked again.

"He's a racist."

"I'm sorry. Is that a crime? Isn't that what someone thinks or believes? I was asking what he actually did to cause you to look for him. Did he commit a crime?"

"We just want to talk to him, that's all. If you do see him, try to keep your distance. We believe he's mentally unbalanced and may be a danger to himself and others. Here's my card. If he comes here, we'd appreciate a call."

"Okay," I replied. With that, they left and I closed the door. As I looked out through my window blinds, I could see them walking back to their car parked a couple of doors up the street. On the back of the car, someone, probably Jack, had painted that strange rounded arm swastika in white paint. When the feds saw it, they turned around to look back toward my place. I closed the blinds. Something had happened to me while Jack was at my place. I was changed somehow in some subtle way. It was as though I had just awakened from a sleep that I had been in for most of my life. Things now seemed very clear. I could see the underlying unity of all things and I could see the separateness of all things. I realized that there really was a struggle going on in the universe between light and dark, but that it was different than the struggle talked about in some religions. Things that some believe are evil, are actually good and things that some believe are good are actually evil. I could just sense it. We are born wearing our uniforms and we are on the side we are on because that's the way God, or the subatomic particles, or a higher force, or nature, or whatever, is ordering the universe. Our goal and our purpose is to survive and move ever higher and make more of us than them so that light dominates and so we can share the consciousness of the source of all. Then again, maybe I caught some sort of contact craziness from Jack. I should have asked him for an objective miracle for proof. So, I imagined him glowing and I imagined sub-atomic particles. Where's the real proof? I went into the basement to make sure crazy, Homeless Jack had closed the window. The odd thing was that it was closed and locked from the inside with a padlock, and there was no other way Jack could have gotten out. But he had. I figure he must have slipped out the back door when I wasn't looking. Next to the window was a piece of paper upon which Jack had written: "I hope you can now see clearly. We cannot find God or our destiny unless we separate out and start the process of becoming a new species truly separate from other human types and incapable of mating with them. We must spread our genes and our Essence by having as many white children as possible, as quickly as possible. God wants these things, and we must obey and carry out His will. There is no other way. Having pure children is God's first law for us. That, and the other things I have received are what God commands. That's the end of the argument. There are none who can argue against God. You're either on the side of God and light or you're on the side of evil and dark. Carry God's symbols with you always. As above, so below. Struggle always and love the struggle. Leave the religions of the humans and accept the religion of God. Leave the death religions of the others. They are not in your blood. Right blood is the foundation, right belief is the key, right action is the way. With these three, and God willing, you shall prevail. Make your choice."

If you run into Jack sometime, don't be afraid of him. He may be crazy, but just humor him. He really thinks he's having revelations. Of course we, being modern people, know that revelations are not to be believed in their own age just as prophets are without honor in their own land. We should get our religious truths from dead prophets and the corporate types in our modern religions because the ever existent God has, for some reason, been silent for a very long time and he doesn't talk to us anymore. Right? Maybe not. Ask Jack.

HOMELESS JACK ON POST-AMERICAN AMERICA

"Look man," said Homeless Jack, "over the past few years the multiracialist propaganda machine has been working overtime in placing columns in various newspapers about Mexican-Americans, Chinese-Americans and others in which the main thrust of the columns is to convince whites—European-Americans—that the massive non-white immigration to this country is a good thing and that these new "immigrants" besides "just looking for better lives for their families" (ain't that the usual hoary cliche, though), are also becomin' good 'Mericans while maintaining their own friggin' cultures. Sure they are. What a bunch of crapola. In fact, what's going on is an attempt to transform America from what it has been for about two hundred years—a New Europe—peopled by Europeans, into a Neo-Melting Pot where distinct human types will be destroyed.

"The truth is that the seeming 'diversity' that is being pushed today, ain't the final result that is sought by the multiracialists. Their ultimate goal is to blend all humans, all nations and all religions into a bland new human conformity, the Tan Everyman. To that end, the resistance of European-Americans to the blending must be broken down in all ways possible. They're throwin' us all in the big masher, man.

"These attempts to break down the resistance are takin' many forms, but in 'Merica today, we're surrounded with these efforts 24 hours per day. It's in advertising, it's on TV, it's in our books, it's in the rewriting of history and science. The elites are tryin' to hide racial differences from the common folk. It's especially big in our schools. It's a massive campaign to make European-Americans blend. Those who blend themselves away are praised—read, given positive reinforcement by society while those not blending are often condemned—read, given negative reinforcement by society. It's Pavlovian conditioning on humans on a massive scale. It's all tinkling bells and slobbering human dogs, my friends.

"How is the campaign working? Like we was a buncha stupid sheep. According to a 1958 Gallup Poll, only 4 percent of whites approved of black-white marriages. By 1994, the number approving of these marriages had increased to 61 percent. Goes to show you that advertising and public relations campaigns are as effective in selling genocide as they are in selling butts."

OURSELVES ALONE

There was a time in America when—yes, it's true boys and girls—"American" was synonymous with white people. Even the Ugly American was a white person and it would have been unthinkable to think of the Ugly American as a Mexican-American, a Chinese-American or a African-American, because they weren't really Americans in the public mind throughout the world, and any Americanness they might have was always trumped by the identifier before the hyphen.

White Americans, however, didn't need any hyphens to describe them. They were just plain Americans. Why should it have been otherwise when the term American meant—without saying it—"white American," or its present synonym "European-American." Most of these European-Americans had a schizoid split from who they really were—their essential selves—and felt no kinship with the "foreigners" in Europe. Thus, a German-American might travel to Germany, but feel no sense of oneness with the people of his blood. They were disconnected. French Americans could visit France and complain about how rude the French were and not even know—in the deeper sense of the term—that they too were French. America could fight a war against the "evil Germans" with a German-American—Dwight D. Eisenhower—at the head of its armies and not even give a second thought to the fact that he was German. The links to the old lands of Europe were blended away in the American Melting Pot which was the term coined to describe such blending of the various European nationalities. The American type was something of a plain wrap European living on the American continent.

Today, America, with massive waves of non-Europeans coming to this land, is what I have called Post American-America. It is a land quickly losing its traditional American.

Oh, you'll still hear some WWII era white Americans saying things such as "Don't put no hyphens in my name, I'm just an American, by gum." That this shows a lack of a sense of identity on their parts and is a smarmy form of racism is missed by most who say this.

A new generation of whites is coming to understand the reality that "American" no longer defines them. And since most whites in the country are the product of several European nationalities, few have any strong glue that holds them to any particular European nation. Those who understand this and whose consciousness has been raised are increasingly seeking their identities in their generic Europeanness and this is leading to ever more incorrect charges of "white racism," against some of these European-Americans who are seeking a meaningful identity that is real for them and gives them an anchor to hold on to.

What national identity, for example, would an American with Irish, English, French, German, and Swedish blood feel comfortable with? The glue is weak to all these nations. What is real and basic to his or her identity, if he or she but understands this, is his or her Europeanness. But, what is European music, dance and art? What is European cuisine? Clearly, each of the European nations has differences in these things.

Ultimately, a European-American is, as I said above, a generic plain wrap European living in America. He is not just an "American" because this does not distinguish him from others living on these shores who are not white, and he's not a European, because he wasn't born in Europe. He's also not Irish, English, French, German, Swedish or any other nationality from Europe. Still, he looks like people from those nations and, even if he doesn't know it, he thinks like them. In Post-American America, whites have to rethink their identity if they wish such identity to be authentic, and whites need to start thinking in terms of Ourselves Alone.

If whites were to make a flag to represent them as a race—as Ourselves Alone—it might be a black field with a tiny little 10% section in white in the center representing them alone in a sea of black. That's the situation of whites on Earth whether whites like it or not. Whites are Alone and we are surrounded by the 90% of humanity that is non-white. despite protestations to the contrary, most of the non-white population of earth doesn't like whites very much and would be pleased if we simply ceased to exist. The multi racialist blenders with their bedroom genocide are trying to make our extinction a reality.

THE GREAT WHITE FATHERS AND MOTHERS

Over 90% of all humans are nonwhite. Fewer than 10% are white. Yet when nonwhites kill whites we often see certain whites rush in to apologize for and even embrace the nonwhite killers. A few years ago a white post-America American girl was murdered in South Africa by blacks. Instead of condemning her killers, the girl's parents actually embraced them.

What psychology is at work in such a phenomenon? Certainly, it must be partly related to the Stockholm Syndrome where hostages take the side of their captors, but it must also be related to a smarmy form of aracialism that has at its core the subconscious belief that whites are better than nonwhites and when the former do anything wrong they must be held to a higher white standard, but when the latter do anything wrong, they were forced to these wrong acts by whites and they are to be treated like innocent children and are to be loved and hugged by the paternalistic and maternalistic, Great White Fathers and Great White Mothers. These Great White Fathers and Great White Mothers among us are able to cover up their psychological problems with seeming dogoodness, and they are often even praised by other Great White Fathers and Mothers for their forgiveness and for their "selfless"work with the downtrodden.

Talk to some of these Great White Fathers and Great White Mothers and if you are discerning you'll fell that you're talking to cat ladies, sans cats, who treat non whites much as cat ladies with cats will treat their cats. They are seemingly selfless in their support of non whites and will be the most vocal in their condemnation of racism. However, when you analyze what they're about you'll realize that they have a subconscious belief that whites are better than non whites and must protect and help them.

Paradoxically, these Great White Fathers and Great White Mothers also seem to have the subconscious belief that non whites are really just whites trapped in dark skin prisons and that it is the God given duty of these Great

White Fathers and Great White mothers to help these inner white people emerge from these dark skins so they can act white. The enemy of the non whites and the Great White Fathers and Great White Mothers are, of course, at least in the twisted minds of the Great White Fathers and Great White Mothers, evil white racists who are trying to keep the inner white people inside those dark skins, because of irrational prejudice against skin color.

When these Great White Fathers and Great White Mothers speak of the content of the character rather than the color of the skin of people, they often mean—even if they don't consciously know it—that the content is white. And, when these Great White Fathers and Great White Mothers talk of diversity, they often mean they want a world that is white in attitude but non-white in appearance. They want a world of black, brown, red, and yellow white people.

This Great White Father and Great White Mother attitude can often be seen both in liberals and main stream conservatives. In the former it is often more obvious and requires no further comment here, but in conservatives it is often seen in the effusive public praise given to non whites when they act white. Check any main stream conservative publications and you'll see some blacks and other non-white being written about in glowing terms for the most mundane achievements. Oftentimes this is just an example of smarmy racism and feelings of superiority held by the Great White Fathers and Great White Mothers who act as though they're school teachers and all non-whites are like children who just need proper encouragement to allow the inner white people inside them out.

If we really look at race and racial attitudes we see that so called white racism and white guilt are a little more complex when one truly looks at them, but few among us will discuss these matters.

HOMELESS JACK ON WHITE LIBERATION

"'White liberation?' What the hell's that and liberated from what?" Well, I'll tell you what. Did the words racist and maybe bigot or similar words pop into your brain when you saw that title above? Did you begin slobbering all over your shirt like Pavlov's dogs? If so, you're not alone. A whole bunch of brain pithed white folks get some kinda reaction when they see words like white liberation. Now, I ain't sayin' you're brain pithed, don't get me wrong. But, you've been exposed to the same propaganda as the rest of us, and it's only natural that your subconscious has some stuff in there that causes you to react negatively about white folks even though you may be white yourself.

"The stupid genocidal propaganda has been hittin' us for at least the last 40 years, amigos. We've been conditioned to run from our essential whiteness…from our genotype…from what we are as determined by nature.

"An indication of the psychological effect of this brainwashing is shown in the fact that the same people who do get a twinge over whiteness don't get such a twinge or uncomfortable feeling when they see a title such as 'Black Liberation.'

"In both cases, the word Liberation is the constant. It is the word "white" that bothers those with the twinge even though they themselves are white. This is often the result of the self-hate and self-loathing that they have been conditioned to feel due to the fact that they have internalized the negative images of whites, put out by white haters. The subconscious is a big deal with humans, man, and it makes you do stuff and think things that your conscious is sometimes surprised by.

"Whites are not the only people in history who have ever experienced this phenomenon, but they are the group that most evidences it today. In the past, we've seen blacks, American Indians and other racial groups express the same type of self-hate toward their own people. Blacks went through a major consciousness raising in the early '60's and have largely emerged from the sickness of the soul that caused them to hate themselves. American Indians are still going through their consciousness raising. Whites are still in the throes of the soul sickness.

"The fact is that many whites are now so brainwashed, that they need to be deprogrammed more than the most brain dead religious cultist. This deprogramming is a start on the road to mental health and to white liberation.

"There it is again: White Liberation. Liberated from what? Many whites look around themselves and see that there are many white faces at the top in government, the media, business and in fact in all fields of human endeavor. So, if whites are at the top and presumably in charge, who or what do whites need to be liberated from?'

"The answer is that they need to be liberated from a system that is working against their best interests and is keeping them from knowing the true freedom that comes from living in a society where the streets are free of non-white violent crime, and where they don't hide behind triple locked doors when the sun goes down. They need to be liberated from a system that won't allow them to have self-determination as individuals or as a distinct people. They need to be liberated from the false ideas and notions of a bankrupt multi racialist ideology that has at its heart the false notion that all man forms are the same except for different paint jobs. They need to be liberated from the current orthodoxy that forces them to have an internal censor lest they think or speak things that may be considered by some to be politically incorrect. They need to be liberated from false thoughts that keep them from feeling a healthy pride in themselves, their people and their heritage. They need to be liberated from the deception that the highest good is for them to blend into the 90% of humanity that is non-white and thus become extinct as a distinct people.

"One step on this path to white liberation is for non-elite whites…conscious whites, for lack of a better term…to realize that there are certain white elites who do not really *know* that they are white, and that many of these white elites practice a smarmy form of noblesse oblige racism whereby they trample all over the rights and interests of conscious whites in order to pander to non-whites.

"From noblesse oblige racism came anti-white programs such as affirmative action and a society wide attitude that it's all right to discriminate against whites and to give non-whites who are less qualified the job or college spot that should have gone to the more qualified white.

"Today, we see the sad spectacle of unconscious white elites leaving their safe gated communities in their BMW's and driving to their safe high rise buildings where they don't have to face the reality that ordinary whites face each and every day of their lives.

Then we see these out of touch unconscious white elites dictate their false notions of the world and of human psychology; learned not on the streets nor on factory floors, and certainly never in the military, to these ordinary whites.

"If the ordinary whites complain about the tyranny and oppression that they are living under at the hands of the unconscious white elites, and of an increasingly out of touch government, they are ridiculed and called racist, bigoted, prejudiced, insensitive and a host of similar words which, in effect, cause many ordinary whites to be silent.

"These ordinary whites need to be awakened to realize that they are a distinct people joined by blood for thousands of years before there ever were any of the present governments, religions or philosophies. They must understand that their interests are often different both from the unconsciousness gene dormant white elites, and from non-whites who do not share their genes and who are not their people. "When these ordinary whites come to this realization, they will start to have their consciousness raised and will start to understand many things in the world that before were only a muddle. When they reach this stage in their awakening they often start to speak up and begin to mobilize to correct the wrongs forced on them by incorrect and deceptive notions.

"This is not an easy process. Those who have an interest in keeping them docile and passive, immediately start calling such whites names and begin the demonizing process that so often isolates those who dare to speak out from others of like mind but who are often of lesser nerve.

"The name calling acts as a negative stimulus and causes people to want to avoid the punishment of being called names as surely as though they were avoiding electrical shocks for making a wrong choice in a psychology lab. This avoidance reaction when coupled with the approach reaction engendered by positive propaganda about the joys of multiracialism constantly works on the subconscious minds of all of us. However, some of us are more receptive than others and are like the easily hypnotized subjects of stage hypnotists.

"Want an example? Most of the violent crime in this country is caused by non-whites. "White communities are far safer than non-white or mixed communities. This is a simple fact. But, how many whites have you heard speak out about this? Probably none. The brainwashing, and fear of being called names, keeps them silent. Instead, you'll hear a constant stream of propaganda about how wonderful "cultural diversity" is. Few will ever question this statement. Ordinary whites should be saying: "Why is cultural diversity so wonderful? What has it done to improve my life and the condition of my family? How has it helped improve the quality of life in my city? In my country?" But ordinary whites don't usually say these things. They remain silent. The propaganda thus goes unchallenged and sits out there to ensnare and deceive other whites in a thousand ways as surely as advertising ensnares minds for particular products.

"So, one of the first things that ordinary whites must do is to raise their consciousness.

"They must see themselves as different (because they really are different) from other peoples who are not of their genotype and who by their very presence are a danger to their continued existence on a planet where whites are in a very small minority.

"They must stop being afraid of being called "racist," or similar terms. They must start acting in their own self-interest and they must recognize friend from foe. All whites are not automatically friends and all non-whites are not automatically foes. Those, of any color, who allow others the right to pursue their individual and group destinies and the right to self-determination may not always be friends, but they are also not foes "Some readers may say that this is all pretty radical. Those who do say this show thereby that they are still brainwashed, because this is no more radical than what was said to and by blacks at the start of the black civil rights movement in the early '60's. Those who can't see this, need to be deprogrammed.

"Many people don't realize that back in the 1960's at the start of the black civil rights movement, there were more Uncle Tom blacks than blacks with a consciousness of their self-worth. When Rosa Parks refused to give up her seat on a bus to a white man, many blacks snickered behind her back and called her names. Those who did this were as brainwashed as are many whites today. Those snickering blacks had internalized the then current propaganda that had made them non-persons the way many whites have become non-persons today after having internalized the now current multiracial propaganda.

"Today, whites are at about the same stage as were the blacks in the early 60's. There are far too many white Uncle Tom's in our society. These are the one's who are saying that affirmative action, which is discrimination against whites, is good and should be saved. These are the white versions of the blacks who snickered at Rosa Parks.

"If there is a difference between the blacks who laughed at Rosa Parks and the white elites who are today snickering at ordinary whites who want to end affirmative action it is that in the case of the blacks in the '60's, most of those who did the snickering were not elites. They didn't have the power to stop the black civil rights movement.

"The white Uncle Toms today, by contrast, are mostly elites. They often have money and positions of authority. They control the main stream media. They control business. They control religious and social organizations. They control government and the courts. "These white elites are often the enemies of ordinary whites. The fact that these elites are white is of no moment since they are often self-haters who project their self-hate on to all other whites. Being self-haters and having power they are able to inflict their neurotic views of the world on ordinary whites. They are able to enact and enforce unjust laws. They are able to tax the white middle class into poverty to redistribute this money to the non-whites that they favor.

"Whether most people know it or not, we are at the dawn of a white civil rights movement in this country. All the various movements that we read about in the newspapers: the militias, the anti-tax fighters, the fighters against affirmative action, the states' rights proponents, the anti-immigration forces, and many more, mostly have white faces. Many of these groups and their members may still be brainwashed and may deny the racial component of their movements, but facts are facts. Those who would deny a racial component of these seemingly unconnected movements only show, thereby, the degree of brainwashing that they have been subjected to.

"In fact, you'll often hear the most brainwashed whites say things such as: "This isn't racial...." You'll also notice that it is usually only whites who will say such things. You'll rarely ever hear a black apologize for being part of something that is overwhelmingly black.

"It's time that whites stopped running from the reality of race. They have denied this reality for more than 40 years, and in denying it they have looked for answers to our crime and social problems in all the wrong but socially acceptable places. Whites have denied the truth. They have lied to others and to themselves about race. They have put themselves in an intellectual prison ringed all about not with razor wire and steel bars, but with boogey man words, such as "racist, bigot, prejudiced, insensitive." Many whites are fear struck at being called one of these terms and will give up the fight to get out of the prison when anyone uses one of these words against them.

"One result of this intellectual cowardice is that whites continue to tax themselves to fund programs that don't work. Headstart is one such program. No one wants to say that blacks, as a group, may not be as intellectually gifted as other racial groups, so we look for reasons why they don't do as well in school. "Can't be lower I.Q.'s can it? Nope. Must be something else, something...er...non-racist. Must be poor home environment. Yup. That must be it. It's a comfortable answer that doesn't mention race or genes. Then, with this politically correct explanation in mind, we take little black children and put them in school at an earlier age than white children.

"Has Headstart worked after spending billions of dollars on it? Not at all. It's been a big failure. And so it goes with all such false programs based on an incorrect non-racial view of man. Look at sports. Many sports are dominated by blacks. The reason is that blacks are often superior in some tasks requiring quickness, strength and speed. Can we say this in polite society? Nope. You see, if we admit these differences between the races, the we are logically led to also admit the possibility that the brain, which is also made of body tissue may be as different as are muscles and bones. If there can be genetic differences in running and jumping abilities, for example, then there can also be genetic differences in the brain.

"Of course, even though we don't admit that blacks have genetic advantages in certain tasks, we know in our minds that it's true, otherwise we might have Headstart sports programs where white kids would overcome their poor sports home environments and show that they too can be great basketball players. Hey, it's not race. It's environment. Right?

"Man, it's time for truth, and it's time for White Liberation, but if you ain't caught on yet, whites have to be liberated from themselves before they can be liberated from anyone or anything else."

HOMELESS JACK ON INDIVIDUALISM

"We got this general idea in this country that we're all a buncha individuals. Now, okay, that's true, but I figure we've taken it too far in some cases and it ain't doin' us any good and is helping lead to our extinction.

"Anyway, Ayn Rand, whose name and photos make her look like a nice Aryan girl, but who was actually born with the handle Alice Rosenbaum, grabbed on to a belief in hyper-individualism like a crack-head who just found a pipe in the gutter. She put a buncha her thoughts together in a philosophy that she called Objectivism, and thereafter railed against all sorts of collectivism—seeing oneself as part of a group of others like oneself.

"In THE ESSENTIALS OF OBJECTIVISM Rand wrote, "Man—every man—is an end in himself, not a means to the ends of others; he must live for his own sake, neither sacrificing himself to others nor sacrificing others to himself; he must work for his rational self-interest, with the achievement of his own happiness as the highest moral purpose of his life."

"While such a view has some appeal to 'Mericans who still think they're some sort of old west prospectors or something it can too easily be taken to an extreme and can lead to the belief that each one of us is an island unto ourselves and that we have somehow almost magically sprung up on with no family, no ancestors, no connection to others who share our essential natures.

"It is a philosophy of me, me, me that can lead to the destruction of the very genetic group from which the one who has this view sprang. It fails to recognize that individuals with this view, as all individuals with all views on any subject are ultimately beholden to the genes that they had no hand in acquiring and which they received simply by being born.

"Some of the main proponents of hyper-individualism, as you might expect, are the super rich in our society. Some of these super rich types have given in to their egos and proclaim to all hearers that they acquired what they have acquired solely because of their own efforts. "Why, son, you too can be as wealthy as me, if you'd only get out of that chair and work as hard as I did. Anyone can do what I did," is one version of what the super rich often say.

"Hey, that's a screwy thought. You damn well know that all 5 billion people on Earth can't be billionaires. The reality is that it takes more than hard work to rise to the top in any human endeavor. It also takes the right genes and it takes the luck of being born at the right time in history at the right place.

"Does this mean that we should just fatalistically accept lower stations in life for ourselves because we think we might not have the right genes? Of course not. Those with the right genes may find certain things easier in certain areas of their lives, but those who don't have these genes can still achieve much with hard work, and certainly without the hard work they would achieve very little of anything. Besides, we don't really know which among us has super-achiever genes until they succeed, and then, their success, as already mentioned, is often a result of various helpful accidents and coincidences in life.

"Bill Gates, who seems to be hangin' on to the title of being the richest man in the world, would probably never even have been heard of had he been born before computers were invented. He was lucky enough to be born at a time when his genes, which apparently gave him a desire and the ability to work with computers, also gave him computers. Had Gates been born a hundred years earlier, his talents might never have been expressed for lack of a proper vehicle to express them. Hell, he might be out here dumpster divin' had he been born just a few years earlier and been drafted and sent to Vietnam and got exposed to Agent Orange like some of the guys.

"But, go further in this talk of genes and you enter the area of race—the great Sacred Cow of our age. A race is composed of individuals who share the same general genotype. That is, the members of a race have enough genes in common with other members of the race so that these genes, when expressed in the form of a human being, bring forth a being who is much more like other beings with these genes than he or she is like other beings who don't share all these genes.

"Skin color, hair color and texture, eye color and eye shape, are just a few of the most obvious of characteristics that are different in different races of man. In addition to these seen characteristics, there are hundreds of thousands of unseen characteristics that are often only recognized when we look at statistics and note that more individuals of this or that race excel in certain endeavors out of proportion to their numbers in the population. When we see such statistical anomalies, it just makes sense to find out why such anomalies exist. There could be a variety of reasons for the statistical results but most of the time, we'll find that the anomalies are ultimately caused by genetic differences.

"Perhaps, however, this direct talk of genes and race is too charged with the negative connotations that have been put on this subject by the aracial bigots and haters in our society who demand that no one talk about genes and race when such talk points up racial differences between different human groups. If these negative connotations tend to close the ears, eyes and minds of those hearing the truth, then perhaps a metaphor will help open them and make the point that might otherwise be tuned out: A man is the result of the recipe found in the genes. Man is sort of a self-replicating and self-mixing cake who is more like others made from the same recipe than he is like those who are made with a different recipe.

"Make two cakes in your kitchen. One cake is vanilla and the other is chocolate (are we being a little too obvious here?). They're both cakes, but they have slightly different ingredients (genes, in the case of living things), and this is shown in the fact that they look and taste different from each other. This obvious truth about cakes is easy for even the smallest child to see. Next, take those two cakes and put them in the same oven (the environment), and they will react to that environment according to their essential natures, as determined by their Ingredients.

"The vanilla cake will emerge a vanilla cake and the chocolate cake will emerge a chocolate cake from the same environment.

If we are then told that because these two cakes are both "cakes" and because they were both baked in the same oven that they are the same, we would probably believe that the person saying this was crazy.

"The truth is that the vanilla cake would have more in common with all other vanilla cakes even if they were baked in different ovens than it would have with the chocolate cake baked in the same oven.

"This is, of course, a very long way of saying that genes matter and they matter in all aspects of our lives and it is important to understand this and not give in to ego and false pride if one achieves much in life, because one is, or at least is enabled in what one is, by genes as they interact with the particular environment in which they find themselves and according to many other factors. In other words, the genes present the potential of what the creature carrying them can do, but the potential is also dependent on the environment allowing the potential to be realized.

"To take pride in being a vanilla cake through one's own hard work is a little like taking pride in being a billionaire through one's own hard work. Wisdom lies in knowing that one sprang from a recipe and that one should give that recipe some appropriate credit for what one becomes in life, and in not setting oneself apart from others of the same recipe out of false pride and ego.

"Meanwhile, some of the hyper-individualists among us are still adorning their offices with pictures of the bald eagle. And these pictures are sometimes accompanied with a slogan that says that bald eagles don't fly in flocks. You have to catch them one at a time. How noble. What a great example of individualism. Of course, the friggin' bald eagle is just about extinct. Perhaps if it had evolved a flock mentality and mated like crazy it would be better prepared to stave off its extinction instead of having to be protected like delicate china."

HOMELESS JACK ON CHINESE ZULUS

"So, you think you know what an Englishman looks like, right?" asked Homeless Jack. "Well, if that's the case, then you've been watching a buncha old English movies on your telly, mate. See, there's been a controversy going on in England for several years about just who is English.

"The seeds of the problem began back in the old empire days with the Raj and all that. At that time the Brits were romping around the world and havin' their way with all kinds of different countries. They were in India and what became Pakistan and in places like Jamaica and a buncha of other places that were mostly non-white. Well, to help dominate the locals, the Brits enacted laws that said all of these folks who were being subjugated had the right to go to England and be citizens. Bloody fat chance of that happening, thought the Brits, after all, how many of the buggers could manage to get rickety old sailing ships and cross the ocean? Blimey, what? Well, times changed, and wouldn't you know it, the friggin' 'Mericans came up with the airplane and then the damn things got bigger and bigger so they could carry hundreds of the natives to Merry Olde in just a few hours. And, by damn, they came and they came and they came. Soon, England was looking like India and Jamaica. It had the same levels of crime and social problems also. The native Brits were now hidin' out in their homes for fear that they'd be attacked by the darkies, and their fear wasn't misplaced.

"Still, many Brits hung on to the notion that an Englishman was a white person. That's the way it had been even before the gloomy place was called England. But, the growing number of non-whites didn't like that, and besides living in an age when their were big jets to carry them to England they were also living in an age when it was easy to brow-beat whites about race and make them look bad because they felt as strongly about their race as some of the dark folks felt about theirs. It was great, horrific theater and it continues unabated as England becomes a brown Third World nation right before our eyes as beaten down white Englishmen and white Englishwomen become ever smaller parts of the population of their own damn island. And, there is no King Arthur on the horizon to save the nation.

"A couple of years ago a report was issued by an organization called the Runnymeade Trust, which claims it is devoted to "promoting racial justice." Now, most white people, possessed of even a little consciousness of their essential identity, know that whenever terms such as "promoting racial justice" are used that what follows is an attack of some type on white people and their culture. And that's what happened.

"A Professor Bhikhu Parekh (Fine English name, old boy, what?), was one of the authors of the report which contends "Britishness, as much as Englishness, has systematic, largely unspoken, racial connotations." (Really? Gosh.) Professor Parekh continues:

"Whiteness nowhere features as an explicit condition of being British (it doesn't?), but it is widely understood that Englishness, and therefore by extension Britishness, is racially coded." (Oh horrors!).

"Okay. So what's wrong with that? The genuine English people ARE white. You cannot really be English and not be white or you don't understand the term. Words really do have meanings. The Germanic tribes that settled parts of England in the 5th century, A.D. were called, in Latin, Angles (It means angels). They were called this because of their racial characteristics including their white skin. Their land became known as Englaland (land of the Angles) and their language was Englisc (of the Angles). In other words, the term for their land was synonymous with who they were as a racial people.

"But what about that other common term "British"? It comes from the Bryttas who were a Celtic tribe who also inhabited England. Like the Angles, the Bryttas were white people.I know, I know, that's very un-PC of them, but that's the way it was. They were born with that horrible white skin. Couldn't help it. Had something to do with genes. Anyway, the Bryttas and the Angles became one. No great leap there, because they were virtually genetically identical anyway.

"Of course, there's nothing unique in a land being named for the people who live there. It's common all over the world. Russia is named after those other white guys, the Rus, who were originally Scandinavian. Go to virtually any country in the world—save, perhaps, much of the new world—and you'll find that they're named after the tribes who built those countries.

"In other words, the name of the land and the name of the people were synonymous. No big deal. Of course that was before the evil genocidal blenders decided they wanted to commit genocide against white people and force them to blend away their whiteness through assimilation into the 90% of humanity that is nonwhite. To help accomplish this goal of killing off all the white people, the blenders, among other things, have been trying to break apart any psychological/social/genetic/cultural/religious glue that causes white people to stick together as white people or to see themselves as a distinct people. One way to accomplish this is to corrupt the language and make exclusive terms inclusive as they're trying to do in England.

"If the English people no longer see themselves as having certain racial characteristics, but include all people who happen to have washed ashore on the island as English, then there would be few psychological/social controls to keep them from breeding with others who are very unlike themselves. They will have been conditioned to not see the differences. So, if a white English person whose white ancestry goes back thousands of years in England mates with a black who is now called English, and has children with this non-English English person, the children, who won't be white, will help take the English down an evolutionary side road that will change England forever. In time, England will not be white at all. Will it still be England? Certainly not as we know England. It may still be called England and the people may still be called English, but it won't be the same. In fact it'll be something like a rose garden with no roses. It may still have an ornate sign reading "The Rose Garden." However, in place of roses there may now be petunias. So, the plot of land is still called The Rose Garden and the flowers within are now called roses, because of the name of the place, but, of course, they are really petunias and not roses at all. Now, don't get me wrong. Petunias are fine flowers, but they ain't roses.

"England's Home Secretary Jack Straw demonstrated how blenders think when he said that Britishness has become inclusive, "with people happily defining themselves as black British or Chinese British." How nice.

"Following that logic, Chinese who are born in Zululand are Zulus and Zulus who are born in China are Chinese. If you go into a Chinese restaurant someday you may be in for a surprise. Continuing with this logic we might then say that in the U.S. we have white Apaches and white Sioux because the whites live on land owned by these tribes. Be careful the next time you buy an authentic Apache or Sioux souvenir, because it may have been made by a white guy whose ancestors may have been white Englishmen. It's a bollixed up world we're livin' in.

"Of course, one suspects that many Zulus, Chinese and American Indians might not like having their essential identities blended away in words, this way. In fact, various Indian tribes, to their credit, are now protesting that their tribal names should not be used as names of sport teams. Meanwhile, few whites are protesting the use of their tribal names—Celtics—for example when used for sports teams. So, what we're seeing in the world today is that whites are expected to be, and are acting the part of, raceless drones with no pride in who they are. They're also expected to commit genetic suicide by blending in with other peoples and to show great respect for the genetic and cultural sensitivities of these other peoples.

"Whites are the punching bags of the planet, dear friends, and much of the punching is being done by whites themselves. So, if you're white, just stand there and let everyone walk up and take a few punches at you, and be sure that you never punch back, because that would be "racist." And to prove how unracist you really are, take a couple of punches at yourself.

"Naturally, if the blenders succeed in killing off all the whites through bedroom genocide and other means, they'll then probably begin concentrating more on exterminating other distinct peoples who have identities other than the lumpen "human." First, they're coming for the white people…then…."

THE NEW CENSORSHIP

Freedom of speech, one of America's most sacred tenets, is coming under fire these days. And, as might be expected, the tyrants who want to tell others what they can or cannot think, read, say, see or write are justifying their tyranny with rationales calculated to fool those who are incapable of critical thinking. One buzz term, which they apply to speech they don't like is "hate speech." What is hate speech? Whatever the tyrants don't like. What don't the tyrants like? Hate speech. You no doubt get the picture of how this little merry-go-round scam works.

These true haters of freedom are succeeding with their repression of free speech in countries whose citizens didn't long ago demand the freedoms that we have in the U.S. and who weren't quick enough to enact their own versions of the First Amendment—the wellspring of all of our freedoms.

In the U.S. it was no luck of the draw that the founding fathers put freedom of speech as the First Amendment to the Constitution, because they knew that without this freedom, no other freedoms could exist. People need to be able to express their views and not fear either the heavy hand of government or of petty private sector dictators. This is basic. All else flows from this.

Unfortunately, there are those among us who keep trying to stomp all over free speech rights when the things said aren't what they like to hear.

Sometime ago, it was announced that one of those self-styled anti-defamation groups formed a partnership with an internet service provider to keep speech, that the anti-defamation outfit doesn't like, off the Internet. To accomplish this, the organization followed the usual pattern of labeling anything it doesn't like as "hate," and let the appellation substitute for critical thinking and the ability of the public to decide for themselves about the nature and characterization of any particular exercise of free speech. In furtherance of this repression of what is often political, social or religious (and thus protected) speech, those who would keep others from hearing or reading what some individual or group doesn't like, will often take an extreme example of speech that may be along the lines of, say, someone writing: "Kill all the (fill in the blank)" then rightly call this "hate speech." But, here's the trick. They then add other types of speech to this "hate speech" column that is not hate speech at all but the expression of a political, religious or social position.

Once the term "hate speech" has been defined by the extreme example, it is an easy thing to convince the public that anything that bears this label is unfit for them to hear or read and that the censors have a right to keep them from hearing or reading it. To name a thing, which is to say, give it a label, and define it, forever conjures up an image in the minds of those hearing this label even when the actual thing now being talked about doesn't fit the definition. For this reason we must be precise in how we define things. To do otherwise is to engage in prejudice, based on labels, rather than on facts.

Censorship must be resisted whether it comes from the right, the middle or the left, and the people, themselves, must be allowed to read and hear various points of view on a wide variety of subjects and not have petty tyrants decide on whether any particular speech is acceptable.

The founding fathers were well aware that petty tyrants would pop up in our society in every age, and they were also well aware that such petty tyrants would often make persuasive and compelling arguments for the censoring of what the petty tyrants didn't like Consider. Not long ago there was a controversy at a college in California over having a class or a lecture on the Kennedy assassination in which, apparently, the speaker has the view that either the government of Israel or agents of the government of Israel or people from Israel were behind the assassination. I say, "apparently" because the public was kept from hearing this lecture or class or whatever it was and was left to wonder not only about what was going to be said, but also about the fact that the person who wanted to say it was kept from doing so (thus are born conspiracy theories). The suppressed talk or lecture or class was labeled "hate," by those who didn't want people to hear it and was then easily dismissed, because, remember, we all know that hate is "Kill all the (fill in the blank)." Instead of mass cries of indignation over this tyrannical prevention of free speech, there was hardly a whimper, and presumably this was just another example of the fear of also being called a "hater" simply for defending free speech. It's just the modern version of what happened during the Salem Witch Trials when anyone defending the women accused of being witches was also called a witch.

It gets worse. Germany's highest court has ruled that German law applies to foreigners who exercise their free speech rights on Web sites that are clicked by freedom loving ordinary German citizens. It appears that some in Germany prefer the sound of clicking heels to clicking mouses so long as it is yesterday's victims now doing the heel clicking.

While you might think that such repression of free speech is so beyond the pale, that few people in the United States would ever think that this is anything but the worst form of tyranny, you'd be wrong.

Perhaps it's time that we opened a Museum of Freedom in the U.S. and had all those people who can't understand the basic principles of freedom go through the museum and learn what freedom really means. Perhaps we need to start giving lectures to very young school children about the dignity of the individual and how our freedom of speech was paid for by the blood of those who founded this nation.

We must never let petty tyrants rise up with noble sounding phrases and justifications to put their iron heels on our freedoms. Meanwhile, while some lefties in this nation still think that they're protecting free speech by listening to George Carlin tapes about the seven words that you can never say on television, which are mostly about bodily functions and sex, the real tyrants are sneaking in and censoring speech about politics, religion and social matters.

REPRESSION OF NON-JEWS

Next to the Bible, the most important book in Judaism is the Talmud. The Talmud is the compilation of oral law that evolved over the centuries. It tells Jews how they should live their lives, down to the most mundane details.

Over the centuries, in various countries, the Talmud was censored, banned and burned so that people couldn't read it. The Catholic Church had thousands of copies of the Talmud burned in Paris in 1240. More were burned in 1264. Then, in 1564 the Church said that the Talmud could be distributed so long as it was censored to remove what some today would call hate speech. References to non-Jews as "goyim" (cattle), for example, were removed as were all negative references to Jesus.

Even with the censoring, much of the hate speech remained in the Talmud, as it does today. A few examples of this hate speech might be instructive. In the Sota tractate, a Christian church is called "Beth Tiflah," which translates to mean either a house of foolishness or a brothel. In "Midrasch Talpioth it says that Christians were created for the sole end of ministering to Jews day and night, and that non-Jews are animals in human form. The examples of this intolerant language abound in the Talmud. If you doubt it, you can read it for yourself.

A Jewish writer once said that the study of the Talmud was prohibited at different times in different lands because it was clear that if Jews stopped studying the Talmud, they couldn't survive. Thus, by destroying the Talmud, one could also destroy the Jews. In essence, this belief about the Talmud and its study being essential to the survival of Jews should be broadened. No distinct people can survive in our world today if they are not allowed to have the words and symbols that are unique to them. This is so, because all humans are dependent on words and symbols in their thinking processes. Keep them from being able to read and express themselves according to their own lights and you destroy them as a people. To repress their free speech rights is to repress them as a people. I belabor this point, because, this is precisely what is being done to non-Jewish white people today.

Under pressure from some groups, the German government arrests German citizens if they raise their arms the wrong way or if they possess certain books or symbols.

In all of the above examples, starting with the repression of the Talmud, right up to the latest repression of thoughts made manifest as words, that some are afraid to let others read, we see the same type of basic fear of freedom and free speech. In addition, we see attempts to destroy distinct peoples by attacking the products of their minds and the symbols and words that help give them a sense of identity.

In all of the above examples, noble sounding rationales were put forth for the destruction of the free expression of ideas. The Catholic Church had such rationales and pointed to the anti-Christian writings in the Talmud as their justification. Today, various Jewish groups point to what they claim are anti-Semitic or hate writings on the Internet.

Hopefully, our American sense of freedom of speech will prevail and America will continue to be a beacon of freedom to the world. However, even now there are those who are praising the repression of free expression in European countries. According to news reports, one Rabbi commended the Germans and the French for their repression of free speech. But, as you might expect, he justified his praise by saying that the Germans and French were dealing with hate, racism and Holocaust denial. Don't be fooled. What they were actually doing was nothing less than stopping their citizens from speaking out or reading ideas that other people didn't want them to speak about or read. In other words, they were destroying their own people by forbidding them from using words and symbols that they wanted to use, just as these very same nations had once tried to destroy the Jews by forbidding the Talmud. Bigots and tyrants don't change. They just change their targets.

How should we look at free expression so that we're not manipulated and tricked into censoring religious, political, social or philosophical thought based on what might sound like a good reason to so censor such thought? Simple. We should take a "content neutral" view of all free expression that does not advocate immediate violence. In other words, when we're faced with any type of expression, we should not presume to look at the writing through our own biased eyes and determine that whatever it is we're reading or seeing isn't fit for others to read. We should, instead, substitute terms to see if what some are trying to censor is really what should be protected speech or expression. We as individuals or as members of various interest groups of like individuals—including religions—have no right to tell other individuals or members of other interest groups of like individuals what they may think, say, write, read or see. We are not Gods. We have no such power over other human beings, and if we try to assert such power, we have dehumanized others and made them our inferiors—indeed, we have made them little more than our slaves, who must do what we think is right.

For example, if we were to read that someone wanted to pass a law to stop students from wearing a Christian cross to school, we should ask if the law also covers Jewish, Muslim and all other religions' symbols. If it doesn't, then the law isn't fair, since it's only aimed at one symbol and one group who believe the symbol can be worn. Okay, so we can probably all agree that this example makes the principle clear. But, wait a minute. Change the terms a little more and say that someone wants to pass a law banning a Swastika. The principle should be the same. If the Swastika is banned, then so too should the Star of David and the Christian cross, and all the rest, be banned. If one is allowed, then all should be allowed. That's what "content neutral" demands.

Switch now to the Internet and the attempts to censor free speech mainly by groups with some Jewish nexus, because they don't like the free speech of some people of other religions. If the expression of thoughts by some non-Jews are offensive to some Jews and if Jews can censor them, then the expression of thoughts by Jews that are offensive to non-Jews can also be censored. We've come full circle and we're back to the burning of the Jewish Talmud because some non-Jews find a book written by and for Jews to be offensive to their non-Jewish sensibilities.

Wisdom dictates that we do all in our power to protect the free expression of ideas in books and on the Internet. Why should we fear any ideas and try to keep people from expressing or reading them? If we don't agree with what some other people think and write, then let us simply write our own views on these subjects and let those who read them, decide which ideas they agree with. Let us determine to be a good and a just people, and let us express our views honestly and with forthrightness, and let us have our ideas do battle with contrary ideas for the minds and hearts of men. Let the best ideas win.

Let us set our minds and our hearts on fighting for freedom; not in trying to repress the freedoms of others. Let us say: Never again…will we allow our free speech rights to be curtailed by those who are different from us in philosophy or religion or world-view or race or ethnicity or nationality.

THE NEW PLANTATIONISM

Increasingly, we're hearing politicians and captains of industry supporting massive immigration because, in their opinions, and as recently said by a U.S. Senator, "we need migrant workers from outside this country to fill the jobs."

The reason we need workers from outside this country to fill the jobs is not usually stated, but the answer is a simple one: We're not producing enough people to fill entry level jobs. And, why not? Partly because the culture of the U.S. and most of the Western World (and, the U.S. can still marginally be called part of the Western World, but that's changing fast) is yuppified, overly materialistic and self-indulgent. In this atmosphere, having children is seen as de classe. "Why daaaaaahling, we're not going to have children. We need a new BMW. Besides THOSE people have plenty of children."

Instead of birthing our own children to take the entry level jobs, we rely on the children of people from the Third World. Given the fact that so many people have now been brow beaten into believing that all people are fungible, there's hardly any notice given to the fact that the children of the Third World aren't the same as the children of the First World. "Ohhhhhhhhh. Racism. Run and hide Mildred, why, sputter, sputter, some of my best friends are…hey, we all bleed red blood you know…why, people are just people." And, how do people know all these "anti-racist" things that have been turned into clichés for the half-bright? They've been conditioned to believe these things. They've been sold on the false idea that people are all the same and that genes don't matter for anything but the most obvious things. Thus, those who buy into this nonsense will begrudgingly admit, because they have to, that people have different color skin. However, they believe that skin color is like paint on a car; something that's applied once the thing itself has been fully made. In fact, however, skin color is just an outward easily seen manifestation of thousands of differences. Are these differences important? Well, in our country, they shouldn't make any difference before the law. All people who are citizens of this nation should be treated exactly the same before the law. However, this doesn't mean that such differences are unimportant to us as beings who want to survive and not become extinct as distinct types.

The point of this, of course, is that people are not fungible. You can't replace all the red ones with brown ones or yellow ones or white ones ("Ohhhhhh, cover your ears Mildred. He said the "W" word) and not change the society.

What we're seeing in the modern world is that natural pressures in society that would normally cause people to have more children, aren't working properly to preserve human diversity, because the pressures are relieved by Third World children, who are seen, remember, as the same as First World children. As time goes on, there is a changing of the genotype in the land as no more little First World children are born. And, as the First World non-parents get old and die off, no one of their genotype replaces them. They are genetic dead ends.

The difference between us replacing ourselves with our own children and what we're now seeing, is a little like the difference between plantations and family farms.

On plantations, the work was done by slaves or indentured servants, while the masters sat back. On family farms, by contrast, there were pressures on the families to have more children to help with the work on the farm. Plantationism was a dead end. Family farms, on the other hand, helped build America, because they supplied the people from within that kept the country growing.

Oh, sure, it's a bit more complicated that this, at least in the telling, but the reality of humans is not much different than the reality of all living animals. When food is plentiful, and there are few natural enemies, animals who eat that food multiply. When the food is scarce or where there are many natural enemies, the animals who eat that food and who are the targets of their natural enemies diminish.

How about with First World humans? We're our own natural enemies. Food is plentiful, but do we multiply? Not as we should. Instead, we kill off our future with various forms of birth control and abortions. But, you may say that there are starving people on the planet, and if WE hold down OUR birthrate, then these starving people may have food. Okay. The problem is that THEY aren't holding down THEIR birthrates. All that you've accomplished with such a world view is to limit the number of your own offspring. And, as already mentioned, you may believe (assuming that you have been conditioned in non-racism) that people are just people, so it doesn't matter if you don't have any children. Your children are the children of others who don't share your genes. The reality, however, is that their children aren't real replacements for you, because they are not you in the sense that your children would be you—as much as a child can be the parent.

Our survival is based upon our reproducing more of our own kind. This means that we need to correctly understand what our own kind really means. The haters who are trying to destroy distinct human types and blend them all together will call this racism, since they are known to define down terms to give them incorrect meanings in order to trick people into committing their own genocide, but those who believe in the laws of nature understand that this is just self-preservation and the prevention of genocide.

We do not need a constant flow of Third World people to fill the jobs of America. We need to drop our immigration to a trickle, and then we need to let the internal pressures build so that Americans will again start having children to fill the jobs. We need to stop acting like Plantation Masters, because to act that way is to accept short term comfort that will lead to long term destruction.

WORKERS OF THE NATION UNITE!

What's this, a call to Marxism? Hardly.

At a time when more and more of America's factories are being shipped to Mexico, the nation is seeing an increasing influx of workers from Mexico who want higher U.S. wages.

Since our factories are now down where they came from, many of these workers—many of them here illegally—are taking service industry jobs. Restaurants and hotels are full of them. Meanwhile, the elites who head up the big U.S. unions are realizing that their strike weapon so successfully used against factories in the past won't work now. Strike a factory, and it's likely to pack up and head down Mexico way. Hasta la Vista Baby. So the unions are hobbled in their attempts to "help" their members, and many of their members are drifting away both physically and emotionally. This is not good for the Union elites whose strength comes from vast numbers of cannon fodder level members.

The answer for the Union elites is to organize in the service industries. After all, you can't move a restaurant or hotel to Mexico. And since, as mentioned above, more and more of the workers in the service industries are workers from Mexico and points south, the Unions are now having to pander to these workers rather than the traditional primarily European-American workers who were once the backbone of the unions.

Who can the European-American workers look to for help? Their traditional ally, the Democrat Party is as culpable in causing the destruction of American factories as is the Republican Party. Furthermore, the Democrat Party has long been moving away from serving the needs of European-Americans in favor of various minority groups. What about the Republican Party? Same story as the Democrat Party, except in the Republican Party there is still a very strong grass roots European-American element that is as disgusted with the realities in the GOP as they are with the elites in the unions and in the Democrat Party.

These grass roots European-Americans are known by a variety of names, including: Reagan Republicans, Reagan Democrats, nationalists, populists, conservatives, right-wingers, rank and file and more. Whatever they're called, these are the folks who are in the forefront of many of the present social movements in this nation. In California they passed Prop.187 (anti-illegal immigration initiative) in a landslide even in the face of being called racists and worse by the usual loopy lefties. They also passed Prop. 209 (anti-affirmative action initiative) and more recently Prop. 227 (English only in schools).

This group has no home in the Democrat Party anymore, but old myths and traditions diehard, and many of these workers cling to the myth that the Democrat Party looks out for them and the Republican Party looks out for the rich. We find this attitude is far more prevalent in the traditional factory cities of the east coast of the U.S. Democrat Party membership has been passed down from European-American worker father to European-American worker son for generations. It's almost like a religion.

If these workers will take some time to consider the new reality of closing factories, immigrants flooding into service jobs and unions falling all over themselves to recruit these immigrants they may come to the realization that their home is with the rank and file in the Republican Party.

Oh, many of these workers will be put off by the elites in the GOP, but they need to know that the elites are few and the rank and file mostly ignores them anyway. In the GOP today, the elites are trying to isolate the activist European-Americans, but the activist European-Americans have long ago isolated the elites. This is shown in the fact that most of the big wins in the GOP are coming up from the bottom and that when the elites don't listen to the rank and file, the elites are deserted.

Also, the GOP is still the home of Pat Buchanan, and if anyone is for the workers of this nation it's this guy. With many more European-American workers in the GOP, Buchanan and those like him can rise to the leadership of the party and transform it into the party that will save your jobs and America.

Now, this isn't an ad for the GOP, and in truth, the best solution would be to have a new viable third party, but frankly, under our system of government it is almost impossible for third parties to ever elect enough people to congress to ever make a difference. If we can get the system changed to be more like those found in Europe, then the above suggestion to join the GOP will be retracted and the suggestion will be to join the new third party.

Workers of the nation unite! It's the elites of both parties who are selling you down the river. These elites can jet off to their factories in Mexico for an afternoon lark, while you're left standing in the ruins of a once prosperous industrial economy.

WE'RE ALL THE SAME?

The standard propaganda line among aracials is that the races of man are all the same except for some minor little cosmetic differences. The reason that many aracials repeat this line is to encourage mixing and mating between the races to create a multi-ethnic Tan Everyman (my term, not theirs). If there are no real differences, then any separation or non-mixing must be the result of prejudice, bigotry (ho hum, yawn) racism.

To maintain the propaganda, the aracials try to hide as many real differences—and there are hundreds of thousands of them—in talk of cultural or environmental causes. The aracials will do mental gymnastics to avoid mentioning any differences caused by genes, because to admit such genetic differences is to be, by definition, a "racist."

Now comes news from the National Institutes of Health that white patients should be treated with one type of surgical regimen for glaucoma, while a different regimen works better for blacks. How can this be possible if the races are the same? Don't ask.

And what about the fact that most police departments across this nation have stopped using a standard choke hold on black criminal suspects because blacks often die from holds that don't even bother whites? Don't ask.

A comprehensive list of the differences between the races would fill a small library. However, the point to be made is simply that such differences exist, and that these genetic differences are primarily what cause the every day differences that we see between the races.

Blacks dominating basketball and certain other sports? Genetic differences that give an advantage in certain tasks. Whites dominating certain mental activities? Genetic differences that give an advantage in certain tasks.

Of course the environment—meaning here, those things outside genes—does play a part. If the rules of different sports, for example, were different we might see different results. In boxing, for example, the rules favor black boxers who can use hand and foot speed to an advantage coupled with less chance of bleeding and a general ability to absorb punches to the chin with less harm than with whites.

Suppose, however, that boxing were changed so that rabbit punches to the neck were the most common punch thrown. We'd no doubt see more blacks being knocked out, because it is this neck area in particular, and the cardio vascular system in general that is the weak spot that makes blacks more susceptible to choke holds, and other attacks to this system.

In this regard, it is worth noting that scientists have recently acknowledged that one of the major health problems with the black population—high blood pressure—is not caused by too much salt in soul food as was once believed, but is caused by genes.

Whites tend to have slower hand and foot speed. Whites cut and bleed much easier (blood vessels closer to the surface), and whites often have glass chins and can be knocked out fairly easily with a right cross on the point of the chin.

The way boxing and many other sports are played gives blacks an advantage over white athletes. The aracials, ever PC, will often say of a black athlete "He's a natural athlete," (read, "We mean genetically, but we don't want to use the word.") while of a white athlete they may say "He's got heart and he really tries," (read," He doesn't have the genes for this sport, but we don't want to say that.").

As in all things in life it is important to know one's strengths and one's weaknesses and to play to one's strengths. This doesn't mean that whites should stop competing in those sports where they are at a disadvantage nor that blacks should stop competing in those areas of life where they are at a disadvantage, but that one should consider genetic differences in all things. And, in the real world there are good white boxers and bad black boxers and there are very intelligent blacks and some pretty dumb whites, because in every racial population where most members of that population are clustered under the center of the bell curve, there are still members of that racial population out towards the lips of the bell where the bell curve of one group intersects with the bell curve of another group. Still, the exceptions do not disprove the rule and the rule is that statistically, we can say that the members of the races of man are generally much more like other members of their own race than they are like members of other races.

It's time to start talking about race with honesty and not with an agenda. The aracials can pretend that racial differences don't exist, but that doesn't change the fact of these differences.

INTOLERANCE, BIGOTRY AND HATRED

Intolerance, bigotry and hatred seem to go hand in hand, and lately we've seen ample examples of these three evils coming from the usual sources who try to browbeat others into submission and to stop others from exercising their rights to free speech and to an intellectual airing of ideas.

All good decent people need to stand up against the intolerant bigots, lest these evil doers be emboldened by the silence of good people. Of course small minded bigots have been with us throughout history and they always seem to be at their shrillest just before a new enlightenment takes over the popular mind.

These bigots were there to call names when it was first proposed that the sun and not the Earth was the center of the solar system. They were there to call names when people said the Earth was round and not flat. In every age, we have had to contend with these anti-intellectual bigots who are afraid of ideas and words that question whatever the current orthodoxy of the age happens to be. In the end these bigots always lose, and eventually crawl back under their rocks because in the end no matter how much they deny truth, truth will always remain truth. It is not truth that will change, it can't. It is as it is. And in the end truth prevails and we go through enlightened periods in our history where intellectualism takes over from the bigots.

Perhaps, today, we are on the cusp of such a new enlightenment—and a new age of freedom where ideas of all types can be floated out where others can read and cogitate upon them—because surely we are seeing the haters at their shrillest these days.

It is always easy in every age to look at intolerance bigotry and hatred from past ages and to believe that we would not have been part of such evil had we lived back then, but when we're faced with evil in our own age, we seem to have a hard time seeing it. This is often so because bigots are rarely the cartoonist characters of children's books. Bigots look like everyone else, and they often make persuasive arguments for their hatred that fools many people.

How then do we sort it out and separate bigots from good people? The answer is that we must listen to what is being said and how its being said. If someone is simply shouting hate terms at others, you may expect that you're dealing with a bigot. Good people don't usually shout names at others and attempt to smear them.

As I've written in other columns—and this should not be a surprise to anyone—the great untouchable subject in our age is not the shape of the solar system or of the Earth but race. And why is this so? Because there is a view that the way to peace and harmony on our planet is to show that all the races of man are identical. One of the problems with this though, is that the subconscious belief in certain secret intolerant bigots and haters' minds is that the basic model human to which all other groups are thought to be identical, is white.

There is an attempt by many of the secret intolerant bigots and haters to shoehorn diverse peoples into a white mold rather than an acceptance of these diverse peoples as unique fully formed peoples standing on their own. Since these secret intolerant bigots and haters—who almost always have white skin—have often set themselves up as patronizing protectors of these diverse peoples, they often get away with their smarmy feelings of superiority. Still, many intelligent people of all races are now starting to recognize in these "protectors" the same attitudes that sent their intellectual forbears on missions to "civilize the natives" by forcing various non-white peoples to act and be white in all ways. Those natives who so acted—those who gave up their native dress; those who covered their breasts; those who gave up their own religions; those who gave up their own hair styles; those who gave up their own cultures; those who gave up their own languages, received positive reinforcement in one way or another from their "protectors," while those who didn't accept the ersatz white man's ways were demonized and often either killed outright or had their spirits broken.

This incorrect view that all people are really white people and only need to be taught the white man's ways needs to be rejected not only because it's wrong, but because it strips blacks, browns, yellows, and reds of their inherent right to their own peoplehood. Furthermore, by trying to shoehorn all other peoples into a white mold, we actually cause the death of many of these people. In my column Black Medicine/White Medicine I discuss just one example of this.

Of course, when we discuss differences we also need to discuss those things that we all share in common. An honest and open approach to both of these would no doubt go a long way to easing racial/ethnic tensions. Isn't it time to accept all people as fully formed people and not just as white people with different color skin?

Unfortunately, present race theory—if we can dignify it with such a name—is one of hiding or pretending that differences don't exist, in the misguided belief that this is the way to harmony. As written elsewhere, this has led to some odd explanations as to why blacks excel in certain tasks rather than the truth that statistically blacks have a natural advantage in certain tasks while whites, reds, yellows and browns statistically each have certain advantages in certain other tasks that are specific to their groups. This doesn't mean, to use a common example, that all blacks are good in basketball or that all whites aren't, or that all yellows are good in math. It just means that statistically, those of one race will plot out on a bell curve as having certain traits and abilities in greater proportion in their population than in other races.

Why aren't all people the same? Why has nature made people in different colors, for example? Because people adapt and evolve to conditions they find themselves in. It's no accident that white people evolved in misty European forests or that black people evolved in hot African steppes.

Humans need Vitamin D. To manufacture it, we must have sun on our skin. Too little Vitamin D is bad and too much is also bad. Suppose you were the great engineer, Nature, (or, God) how would you design humans to live both in forests and steppes? Well you might give the ones in the misty forests white skin with blood vessels closer to the surface so that more sun would get in to manufacture Vitamin D. On the other hand you might give the ones in the hot steppes darker skin to keep so much sun from getting it.

Now, the sun is just one of millions of factors that you, as Nature, (or God) must consider and design for. Your design also has to catch food and stay warm. On the steppes, speed to catch far distant animals would be a plus and long limbs would help keep you cool in the hot climate. In the cold forests, speed is not as important, but preserving body heat is, so you might make a design that has a more compact body style with shorter limbs.

And so it goes as Nature designs and redesigns as needed. Of course, Nature is limited in its designs by all the factors, and more, that engineers designing cars, buildings, planes, bridges or anything else also must face. It's always a trade off in designing things. Say you want to design a warplane. You need to make it light so it can fly. But light means that you can't cover it with armor plate to repel missiles. It would be ideal to give the plane both speed and armor capability, but you can't so you compromise.

So it is with Nature designing living things and people. Nature is limited by many forces as to what it can put in the final design. If you give the human model quick reactions like a house fly, you'll have to hardwire more nerves and muscles to the brain and dedicate more of the brain to this task. This means that you'll have to give up something else in the brain...perhaps some of the higher thinking functions. If you give the human model, too large a brain, its skull will have to be larger, and if you do this a whole chain of changes must be made to the human model. For example, with a larger skull, you'll have to redesign the human female anatomy to be able to give birth to a larger headed baby. It goes on and on. One little change in the design here means that you have to make changes all over the blueprint.

Another example of this design business can be seen in weaponry used by various armies. Fighting a war on a vast open plain would require rifles that are long and accurate at great distances. A short machine gun would be useless, because you'd never hit the distant enemy. Take that army, however, and put it in jungles and the long rifles would be almost useless as they'd get tangled up in the brush. Besides, the enemy is only a few feet away. Here, you need the short machine gun.

Good people should reject the secret intolerance, bigotry and hatred of those who have subconscious beliefs that they are superior to other peoples and who often manifest this secret intolerance, bigotry and hatred in words and deeds that on the one hand causes them to use hate speech against white people who reject their false paternalistic notions towards other peoples, while at the same time these secret intolerant, bigoted haters treat other peoples as little children who must be taught to be white.

BETTY CROCKER GETS BLENDED

In George Orwell's Animal Farm, the animals put a Constitution on the back wall of the barn where all could read it, and thus be assured that their rights were protected. However, each night the evil pigs would sneak in and change a few words here and a few there, so that as time went on, the Constitution that had said that all animals were equal was changed so that the pigs were in control. The pigs' plan worked because the rest of the animals were slow witted and didn't catch on to the subtle incremental changes in the Constitution. Soon the pigs were in charge and they imposed their world view on all the animals.

In many ways, things similar to what happened in Animal Farm are happening in our society. The examples of this would fill volumes, and they have, but this being real life, as opposed to fiction, there are other, even more ominous, permutations to this incremental changing of words and images to manipulate others that we are faced with. Sure we see our rights being trampled on and taken away much as in Animal Farm, but in Animal Farm the animals were at least allowed to remain as they were, and it wasn't their essential natures that was being denied them.

Not so with us in the present Post American America. While many patriots are spending all their efforts in fighting against such things as gun control, the real danger is not in losing their guns, but in losing who and what they truly are. Gun control pales in comparison to gene control, and that's what seems to be going on as some people seem to be intent on ridding the world of the present races of man in favor of a blended new human which we can call the Tan Everyman.

One example of images being changed from what they were to something different can be seen with Betty Crocker, the fictional character used by General Mills on certain of its products. Now, no one is suggesting that General Mills is behind any efforts at blending people, but when society as a whole starts to push any concept—such as blending—then commercial firms such as General Mills are quick to change their own images in order to sell more products, and this gives us, at least in this case, an easy to see example of the blending of America that is going on.

Betty Crocker, as you may remember, used to be a light haired, blue eyed, white skinned European looking woman. Now, Betty has been blended. The Neo-Melting Pot beckoned and Betty was pushed in. Blended away were those now unfashionable European features. Betty has become multi-racial and is now a Tan Everywoman...the new model human that seems to be the goal of the Blenders (of course, they don't call themselves that, and there's no membership in any group that they all belong to, but the Blenders are united in and by a common world view).

Take a look at the new Betty on packages of cake mix and you'll see at least one version of the Tan Everywoman that some people seem to be trying to create on the American continent through all means possible.

But, Betty Crocker is fiction. What's going on in the real world? All the propagandists and tyrants' tricks are on display in the attempt to create this Tan Everywoman and Tan Everyman. I have written about other aspects of this in other columns, but for now simply consider the present immigration policies of this nation. Those who control immigration appear to be treating different peoples like ingredients in a recipe. "Oh, it's still too white, throw in some black...no, that's too much, add a little yellow...hmmm...a pinch more brown...no...add a little red." European immigration to America is minimal—there are still too many Europeans here, for the tastes of the Blenders—so third world immigration is encouraged.

As illustrated with the new blended Betty Crocker, the Tan Everywoman isn't quite this and not quite that. She's a white, black, brown, red, yellow, blend.

To develop the new blended Betty, General Mills took photos of 75 different women of all ethnicities and digitally blended the women's photos together, apparently taking the best features of all, and then sent the result to a painter to complete the blending. The result was the new very PC, multi-racial Betty. According to news reports, Tan Everywoman Betty's teeth and eyes are primarily from an African-American woman from Orange County California. Betty's skin color is a sort of Hispanic brown. Her hair is straight and black and might be from an Asian or Hispanic or maybe a Native American. There's something vaguely European with a touch of Asian about her bone structure, however, as though the Blenders started with a basic European model and then added some darkness to the skin and widened the nose a little, and just adjusted this or that feature a little.

Because Betty's creators had absolute control over the final results, the attractive and friendly looking multi-racial Betty is probably an ideal that will rarely be achieved in real life. It's interesting to note that the Nazis were often excoriated for their alleged attempts to breed perfect (as they defined the term) human beings, but the present breeding attempt with a different, more PC version of perfection is largely ignored or thought to be benign.

The truth, however, is that many of the same people who are often heard to tout "diversity" don't really want diversity at all, they just want a conformity of genes, religion and society. The Brave New World dreamed of by the Blenders will apparently be peopled by Tan Everyperson drones who all look, think and act alike.

Have you ever thought that the people of, say, Japan all look remarkably alike? Wait until the Blenders get finished first with the U.S. and then with the whole planet.

Does this conclusion seem a little over drawn? Those who believe that this is what is going on could point to many examples as evidence of this blending attempt and some would suggest that we should consider the actions of the federal government at Ruby Ridge as one small scene in the attempt to force a Tan Everyman orthodoxy on America.

As you may remember, a small army of Feds attacked the Weaver family in their own home. What was the real crime of Randy Weaver that caused the Feds to take the actions that eventually led to the killing of Randy's 14 year old son and Mrs. Weaver? Was it all about a sawed off shotgun? That was the excuse used by the Feds. But why send in all those troops and snipers and helicopters and tanks over such a relatively minor thing? It just doesn't make sense to those who see something bigger and more sinister in the actions of the Feds. That is, unless you consider the Weavers' beliefs, as the real reason for the attack.

And just what were the Weavers' beliefs? They apparently believed that the races should not be blended. but should remain different as God, in their view, intended.

Their beliefs, they would no doubt tell you, are grounded in their religious views and not in hatred, as is portrayed in much of the compliant me-too media. In other words, the Weavers and others who believe as they do, were and are actually proponents for true diversity, if I understand their views correctly.

Unfortunately, this made those with such beliefs a target for the Blenders, and it was just a series of coincidences, and the whipping up of public hysteria by anti-white bigots that caused the Feds to set up Randy, instead of some other whites, and send in a small army to attack this family minding its own business. The Blenders wanted to set an example of what happens when you dare to challenge the current Tan Everyman orthodoxy, and the Weavers were the example. The message was comply and conform or die.

Why do the Blenders believe that a Tan Everyman is a desirable goal for mankind? The answer is that they believe that there are no real differences between the races anyway and if observable seeming differences can be erased, that potential racial conflicts can be avoided. After all, it's hard to feel allegiance to any particular racial group if you are a blend of all of them.

So, certain Blenders want all the sheep...er..."all the good sensitive forward looking" people to line up and jump in the Neo-Melting Pot, and take a giant leap for the new humanity. "Ve vill create a Superman...an Ubermensch...a Master Race of Tan Everymen to rule the World! All Hail the Tan Everyman. Ve vill all be the same in all things."

Now, if the impression has been given above that there is some sort of Blender Fuhrer along with smoke filled rooms of conspirators, dispel that belief. All it takes is a few active true believers in Blending to get the ball rolling, and then with the right propaganda, many more people will soon develop a vague positive belief that what the Blenders want is good. This is the way it is with many mass movements as the few true believers—often called the vanguard—manipulates people around to the views held by the true believers.

Far fetched? Look around you in our society and see if you don't see lots of seemingly unrelated little things that add up to the creation of a Tan Everyman. For starters, take a look at your box of Betty Crocker Cake Mix.

The real battle in this world may be shaping up as one between those who want to blend all peoples together, and those people, of all races, who don't want to be blended and who will resist the blending and the homogenizing of mankind in order to preserve what they may believe is their unique and valuable genotype.

Eloi and Morlocks?

There is something unseemly about people from one group telling people from another group how to think, live and comport themselves. Many European-Americans don't seem to understand this since most of these people have had their brains pithed with the propaganda of the Blenders and this causes them to not see different peoples as essentially different from them. These identityless European-Americans have become aracial, apolitical, and areligious drones. They are a blah people full of self-hate, self-doubt and ennui. They live but are not fully alive. Not seeing themselves as different from other peoples allows other peoples to manipulate them as though these other different peoples are just the same as them and are acting in their mutual best interests. In fact, there are often very different interests between the groups.

Having been forced to give up their natural sense of identity as European-Americans, many European-Americans seek to substitute false senses of identity to give their lives meaning. They will seek meaning in identities from everything from their love of a particular sports team to their jobs, but will eschew looking to what is essential in their natures for their identity lest they be "racists."

Given the nature of most European-Americans—Europeans who have become generic Europeans living in America—and given the history of the last 200 or so years there is much confusion among them about identity and this confusion is often used against them to their detriment.

In fact, the best thing that could happen to preserve the interests of European-Americans would be for them to find their sense of identity—their peoplehood—in this generic European-American identity. There is little else that is real and genuine for them. All other identities (and we all have many identities) are transitory and artificial. Only the identity that results from the genes is real and genuine. A genotype cannot be changed like a nationality or a job or a religion.

If European-Americans do find their identity in this most basic of all identities then they could be a political force that would ensure their continued existence as a people—a group of individuals who are of the same genotype. Once, a people was synonymous with nation, but now that all nations are being forced by a blender mentality and spirit of our age to be multi-racial, a people must be synonymous with genotype. The old law of the land must give way to the law of the genotype. If European-Americans fail to find their identity as European-Americans then they may be assimilated into the lumpen undifferentiated mass of humanity that they fail to see as different. They will cease to be. They will be extinct. They will have been the victims of genocide and ethnic cleansing.

European-Americans are not the first distinct people in history to be faced with the prospect of their genocide, but they may be the first in modern times to find that their real identity is not really rooted to any particular piece of land but to genes. If the land where they presently find their identity were to fall away—still they would be as they are, because a people is founded on genes not land. A people is a family, a tribe, a nation no matter where it lives. This is something of a new concept for most European-Americans who have for the most part been a landed people. However there are others, Gypsies, for example, have for centuries, been a landless people who have survived numerous attempts to have them assimilated into other populations.

And in the past, various European tribes wandered as cohesive peoples only to eventually settle in lands which they then called by their names. Russia, as you may know, and by way of example, was named for a tribe named the Rus. And although as the centuries have passed and the Russian people have identified with the land, they were and are the same people without the land. They are still the Rus even if every one of them picked up and moved out of what is now called Russia.

To repeat, however, when European-Americans do try to find their identity in their genotype they are often called "racists," and many will recoil rather than brave the social ostracism that accompanies this word. People of other races, however, who find their identities in their races and who are often praised for their black or Latino or this or that "pride," will with one breath tell you how important it is for them to feel unity with others like themselves and in the next breath will call whites who try to do the same thing, names.

And, whites who have, as a group, been the victims of the biggest brainwashing program in history are mostly only too willing to confess that yes, they have had racist thoughts—even though they don't know what is meant by "racist," and like so many of the masochistic types we hear calling into certain psychobabble radio talk shows they will then be freed from their heavy sense of guilt at having been born white, and they will be accepted back into humanity.

We might even say that the all pervasive anti-racist blending propaganda in our society has generated a group Affect disorder among many European-Americans. The victims of this disorder are bland, lifeless and almost mindless people reminiscent of the Eloi in H.G. Wells' THE TIME MACHINE.

As you may remember, the Eloi were child-like androgynous creatures descended from the leisure class who were weak and unable to fend for themselves. The Eloi lived out their lives in garden like settings above the ground ("On top") with few cares except for the nightly incursions of the cannibalistic Morlocks who were descended from the working class and who would emerge from their dank tunnels ("Kept down") below the Earth to eat the defenseless Eloi one by one.

In our society, haven't we all heard a Morlock sort of whisper from many non-whites as some of these people have said that it was they (non-whites) who cleaned the toilets, washed the floors and changed the diapers for whites who were too weak and decrepit to do these things for themselves? This stereotype of whites finds voice in many ways both subtle and gross, and most of us have heard such expressions perhaps without realizing what we've heard, or that we're being insulted. Some of these things take a moment to decode, but once you've developed the ear you can easily hear them. One obvious expression is "White men can't jump." What's really being said in that coded expression goes beyond basketball and means that whites (Eloi) are weak and can't compete with stronger blacks (Morlocks) in physical activities.

The truth is, that in much of the non-white community, whites are seen as sissified yuppies incapable of physical labor very similar to the Eloi. Unfortunately, as with many stereotypes, some of this is true. We have, as European-Americans, developed within our midst our own effete class similar to the Eloi. Our Eloi are mostly elite soulless drones who have been gifted with the ability to climb high in society either as a result of the genes they themselves inherited or as a result of the genes which enabled their forbears to achieve much and hand it down to them. They are what they got from the gene pool, but in their arrogance and ignorance they often tend to discount the value of these genes and assume that whatever they achieved was as a result of their "hard work."

Unfortunately, it is the bloodless dried up thinking of our own Eloi which holds sway in much of the white community and it is their life denying philosophy that has come to define white people. It is a way of thinking that is against all that is vigorous, expanding and full of life and for all that is weak, contracting and which reeks of death. This philosophy is anti-life. It is against all that is new and young and potent. Instead of smiles, it brings frowns. Instead of spring, it brings winter. Instead of joy, it brings sadness. It is an old age home instead of a children's nursery.

So we struggle on with elites who believe, and who demand that others believe, that genes aren't important, and who even hold in contempt the mere thought that genes are important, and who then give little thought to actions they may take that will destroy the very gene pool from which they drank and which has made them what they are. Oftentimes they will even insult European-American non-elites who share their heritage who have not become elites in society and they will often use these non-elites as cannon fodder in wars and as patsies in all manner of ways.

And the elites, while busy destroying their own people, will at the same time pander to various other peoples.

Why is this so? Beyond the psychological aspects of this, it is also partly because of our democratic form of government that was founded when the nation was essentially racially homogenous and when one person, one vote actually meant that all the "one persons" who voted would be the same type of people and who could therefore be expected to vote for their best interests which would be identical with everyone's best interests.

Today, however, in what I have called Post-American America, these elites—these Eloi—pander to the Morlocks and others in order to remain in power and these elites will gladly sacrifice common European-Americans to the ravenous appetites of the Morlocks in order to maintain this power, even though eventually the Morlocks will eject the Eloi as we have seen in recent California elections where the pandering whites have been turned out of office by the very people they pandered to with liberal immigration policies once these other people gained enough voters in the state via the policies of allowing virtually anyone who can crawl across our borders to become citizens.

But of course, the cartoonish versions of Eloi as being apathetic mindless drones and the Morlocks as being murderous mindless drones are not really found in our world, but fictional metaphorical characterizations, if not taken too literally, can sometimes help us to see some truths of our existence.

ENDING BIGOTRY AND INJUSTICE

Bigotry—and let's use the word here to also mean hatred and ignorance—is found among all people and it is always disgusting to see. White people, as we all know, are often charged with being natural bigots and one wonders, when we observe society, if there isn't some truth to this.

However, the bigotry among white people is more complex than what is usually portrayed in the press where whites are shown as cartoonish haters of all non-whites, because, in fact, the roots of this bigotry exist in the subconscious minds of certain people and finds its expression against different targets as the years pass. The targets of the bigotry are always made into acceptable targets by the intellectual currents in either the local society of bigots or in the larger society. Bigotry is enabled by public opinion—which in turn is formed by those who control information. The bigots are simply following the herd in their bigotry and are often seeking a sense of self-worth and acceptance by expressing their bigotry.

This need of the bigots, who are often small minded and intellectually deficient people," to be someone" finds some odd expressions that one may miss if one doesn't know what to look for. For example, a few years ago when the JAW movies were popular, newspapers in coastal areas were suddenly full of stories of "brave" men who had killed sharks. Oftentimes the sharks killed were about the size of the family dog and were about as harmless. Still, the public had been whipped up to go get THEM. After the movie publicity had died down, the sharks were once again largely left alone. But you may be saying,"That isn't bigotry." I say it is, at least in its wellsprings in the mind. In other times and places THEM were "witches" (more about them in a moment) or blacks or Jews or gays or this or that group. Today, THEM is often white people themselves.

A couple of years ago, a white man in Virginia. was convicted of burning a cross. The jury that convicted him was all black, right? Nope. The jury was all white. Well, the guy probably put the cross on some black homeowner's lawn, right? Nope. He and some friends burned it on private property, with the permission of the owner, away from houses.

So, why was he convicted? Some would say it was because of the new "anti-racism" bigotry in post-American America that blinded the jury to the principle of free expression. Had this guy burned an American flag, he probably wouldn't have been convicted, because that free expression is, if not universally PC, at least free of racial overtones. Furthermore, had this guy been black instead of white, the cross burning probably would have been okay.

He was essentially convicted for the content of his expression and the color of his skin and this is wrong in a society that believes in free expression and equality.

What we're seeing in America is the manipulation of emotions to force natural bigots to simply change their targets. The old bigotry aimed at blacks or gays or this or that group hasn't gone away, it's just changed its target to new acceptable targets of bigotry—whites who express white consciousness and who have been demonized in the press for this consciousness. Bigots don't change, they just change their targets.

And what about the witches? Well, recently a judge in Williamsburg, Virginia denied a witch the right to marry people who belonged to her coven. In case you don't know, Wicca is a religion based on various sorts of old European nature based beliefs and practices. Under our Constitution, this religion should be treated the same as any other religion and the denying of full status to this religion is just plain wrong.

A fair reading of the convictions of the white guy and the cross and the denying of the Wiccans their rights can only lead to the conclusion that bigotry and injustice are still with us.

One expects that in both of the above cases, a higher court will overturn these rulings as being unconstitutional. If the United States stands for anything, it must be bedrock principles that are applied equally to everyone and which protect everyone from small minded bigots.

IMMIGRATION AS GENOCIDE

Multiculturalism is not really an attempt to stay "multi" but rather seeks to first break down resistance among ethnic, racial and religious groups so that a mass blending of different groups will take place in a sort of Neo-Melting pot so that what will emerge, in the view of those pushing the idea, will be a one-size-fits-all new human which they believe will be a good thing and which those who think about the concept a little realize will not be good at all but amounts to genocide. I have called their hoped for universal human: the Tan Everyman.

To understand what multiculturalists and multiracialists (two terms that are, themselves, blending together) are about, one needs to understand that many of the most vehement "multiculturalists" are white elites in our society who hold to a smarmy form of secret racism that says that skin color doesn't matter because underneath all those black, brown, yellow and red skins is a white person just fighting to get out. I call these people Blenders. One of the most prominent Blenders in this nation appears to be none other than former President Clinton. Remember his rationale for bombing Kosovo? He wanted to stop the Serbs from having a country that was 100% Serb.

In the view of the Blenders, it is often evil white racists who are trying to keep those inner white people penned inside their skins because these evil white racists harbor illogical and hateful biases against these skin colors. To stop this, the Blenders want to do away with distinct races, ethnicities, religions and nationalities and have everyone share genes with every other group so that in the future, all humans will look alike and think alike and those sharp distinctions of color and belief will be blended away into a light brown plain wrap human.

Blenders have been with us throughout history. We saw their handiwork with the Native Americans when they forced little Native American children into missionary schools to learn to be white in all ways. We saw the Blenders in Australia when they stole Aborigine children and put them in white families to learn to be white. Like some sort of human phagocytes, the Blenders try to assimilate or absorb other peoples into their collective being; first culturally and religiously and then genetically.

In America today, the Melting Pot myth is being used to help the blending. The Blenders like to preach that America is a great Melting Pot and that we should all blend together as they said we did in the past. The truth about the old Melting Pot is that it only blended genetically similar Europeans together in America. All that was blended away were sharp national differences. The reality was that there were never really any major genetic difference between, say, Germans who came to this country who had lived on one side of a road in Europe in a nation called Germany and the French who had lived on the other side of the road. Europeans were all the same people. In America they became a European Everyman.

Today, the Blenders especially want to blend ethnic and genetic differences in the Neo-Melting Pot. One suspects that the unbridled immigration of non-Europeans to these shores is an attempt by the Blenders to increase the genetic blending. It's as though the Blenders are cooks in the kitchen. "Hmmmm. This is still a little too white. Let in more Hispanics. Hmmmm. We need a little more yellow. Let in more Asians. Now, it's getting a little too light. Let in more Africans."

What the Blenders bring to the world is genocide via the bedroom chamber that is as long lasting as genocide via the gas chamber, and the Blenders will never have to fear being charged with crimes against humanity for their genocide.

Have doubts that bedroom genocide works to kill off distinct peoples? Where did many of the missing Native American tribes go? They weren't killed off so much with white men's guns as with white men's genes as they were assimilated and absorbed into the then expanding white mass. The old Melting Pot was full of white Europeans. Native Americans, because of their small numbers, were no more than spice in the pot, and they soon became whites. Today, the same type of assimilation and absorption is being attempted, but given modern transportation and demographic trends along with the above mentioned Blender belief that all people are really white people under different color skins it may be the white genotype that will be the first to be assimilated, and like the missing Native American tribes, disappear.

The Last of the Mohicans may have to be retitled The Last of the Europeans.

THE MADMAN

Once, during a light rain, he was walking in a run down part of the city and he came upon a Madman. The Madman was a skinny white man about 70 years old with a long dirty beard and long hair underneath a dirty dark green watch cap that covered his head down to his ears. He was dressed in clothes of that dirty skid-row color that's not quite a brown, and which started off as a different color. His pants were many sizes too big for him and they were cinched with a rope. On his right forearm there was an upraised area of flesh that looked like a cattle brand in the form of a spiral. Around his neck he had a little chain and on the chain was a little amulet in the shape of a cow's head.

All the rest of the people, even the other homeless people, avoided the Madman and kept walking along giving him a wide berth. For some reason, unknown even to him, he stopped and listened as the Madman spoke to him. "Why are you talking to me?" he asked the Madman.

"Because, you're listening to me, and you're not turning away," came the reply.

Here is what the Madman said.

"Wait until the cows come home, boy. Wait until the cows come home. You may not buy this, but there's more to this white racial thing than anyone really knows. There's a cosmic element to it. I know this because once when I was living in straight society like you I was with a bunch of people on a sort of hill out in this little wooded park when it suddenly started raining. Everyone ran for cover except me. For some reason I just stood there in the rain as the wind came up twisting all around and blew the rain in my face.

God spoke to me from the blowing swirling wind, saying, "Behold what I have wrought." I looked and I saw such darkness that I thought I had suddenly gone blind. Then way off in the distance I could see a tiny point of light in the darkness and the light moved and it seemed to vibrate as though it was jumping up and down and to each side a little, and it grew larger and larger and larger.

And God said: "I am the One behind the light and the light is My steed. Where there is light, there am I. I am here and I am there at one and the same time. Before there was light, I slept. I awoke and I willed Myself into being from out of the darkness and I devour the darkness. I was before I was. I am the enemy of darkness. I am all struggle and effort and without these I am as the darkness, for the darkness is existence in the absence of struggle and effort. Light and white require struggle and effort and without struggle and effort they cannot exist."

Suddenly I was looking at a village full of black people. Then another and then another. I was shown village after village of black people. It was as though I was flying low over the Earth looking down at hundreds of villages. All were full of black people.

That view changed and I was then looking at a vast grass covered plain partly covered with snow and on the plain were herds of cattle. Not the kind of cattle or cows you're used to seeing, but long horned, really big cattle with what looked like splotches of fur all over them.

And among the cattle I could see men with long staves herding the cattle. I looked, but I couldn't see the faces of these men because they had some sort of dark cowl type of hood over their heads. I could only see their very pale white hands holding the staves. These drovers were herding these hundreds of thousands of cattle across the plains. I watched. Then I couldn't believe my eyes. I was suddenly transported up close to one of their camps where they had some sort of odd tent dwellings. In front of the tents was a cow about to give birth. My eyes were transfixed to this. Here's where it gets really strange, because when the cow gave birth, it wasn't calves that she gave, but little white human babies. There were six of them born from this one cow. One of the drovers took each baby, cleaned it off and gave it some milk from the cow. He then took each one inside the tent.

As I watched, I saw a series of images that rapidly changed in front of me. I saw the words "argent, Angels Aryan, Armageddon Cow Born, aliens, ice, golden calf, goyim. I saw hundreds of centuries pass.

I saw a land that was covered with ice and snow where the sun was dim in the sky and the sun did not look like our sun at all. I saw a dawn that did not look like our dawn. I saw a sun set that did not look like our sunset. I saw stars in the sky that did not look like the stars in our sky. I saw a war and I saw a group of people leave their homes for a far away new home. I saw that they were few in number and their new home was full of people unlike them. I saw that they wanted to make this new land theirs by multiplying their numbers but they had too few women among them to efficiently and quickly do this. I saw that they devised a way to put their eggs into cattle and have them carried and incubated by the cattle until born and that the babies born of the cattle had no intolerance to cow's milk, like the black people. I saw their numbers increase by using cattle as their living birth machines. I saw that soon they were populating large parts of the colder areas of the planet where the sun was dimmer and where they had more protection from its harmful rays.

I then saw that some of the people were mating with the black people and many of the black women were dying because their birth canals was not large enough pass the larger heads of the white babies being born, but those that were born shared some of the characteristics of the whites and some of the blacks and I saw that God was angry, and that God destroyed the Earth. And I saw this repeated several times with the same result each time.

And God said to me: "Look and learn and go forth and teach what you have learned, for I shall soon destroy the Earth again because man is so arrogant that he does not follow My laws." And with that I saw a great destruction of the Earth and then I saw the grassy plains again and once again upon the plains were vast herds of cattle.

I sold my home and car and headed for a city where no one knew me and I've been moving and teaching ever since.

Funny thing. After God spoke to me, I discovered that I had this welt on my forearm and it's never gone away. I think He put it there to always remind me of my mission and to be a sign to me that I didn't just imagine all this.

One thing. Remember what you asked me when I first started talking to you? You said, 'Why are you talking to me?" and I said "Because you're listening to me and you're not turning away." Those are the same words I said long ago on that little hill when God spoke to me and that's how God replied to me."

He had heard enough, and as he was starting to move away from the Madman he heard the Madman yell at him "Wait until the cows come home. Just you wait until the cows come home." As he walked on, he felt a pain in his right forearm as though he was being burned. He quickly rolled up his sleeve and there was a spiral brand, new and red and angry.

When he turned back, the Madman was gone. He suddenly had a craving for a glass of milk.

DISAPPEARING PEOPLES

There was yet another story appearing in a California newspaper some time ago about a lost Indian tribe named the Los Gabrielinos.

Why should such stories be of interest to European-Americans with any sense of consciousness? Simple. The disappearance of distinct peoples through assimilation in the past gives examples to us of what happens when a smaller population of distinct people blends into a much larger population of people unlike them. In a world where white people are only 10% of the human population, and where, thanks to modern mass transportation and demographic trends, formerly insulated pockets of mostly white people are being swamped with massive numbers of the 90% of humanity that is non-white, there is a danger of extinction.

Add to this the Blender ideology that says that it's good to blend together and you start to understand how the Indians disappeared. Their experience may be our experience and we may see the extinction of white people one family at a time. One prominent example is the Bush family. As you may know, Jeb Bush, the governor of Florida is married to a Mexican woman and has children who Jeb's father, former president George Bush, once referred to as "those little brown ones over there." Indeed, the Bush children don't look like Bush children at all, and one Mexican-American columnist once wrote a column that he was struck by the fact that he looked remarkably like one of the Bush children when he was the same age as the Bush kid. And he's right. The Bushes have started to be assimilated.

In the article about the Los Gabrielinos we read about how a woman, who believes that she has some Los Gabrielinos blood, pores over old Spanish records tracking her bloodline into prehistory. What she finds are full blooded ancestors intermarrying here and there until finally they're really no longer Indians at all.

That's part of the problem. You see, the Los Gabreilinos must now prove that they exist in order to obtain some federal benefits allowed only to Indians, so they're trying to reconstruct their past and prove that even though some may now only have a few drops of Indian blood left due to all the intermarrying, that they are, in fact, Indians.

It's really a tale of genocide through assimilation, or in PC terms, through intermarrying, but the story in the newspaper doesn't talk much about genes. Instead, it misses the real point and focuses more about things such as Spain subjugating and taking the Indians' land and shattering their culture. It would have been more honest if the article had said that the Spaniards had shattered the Indian genotype which, of course, is upstream from the culture and is what caused the culture to come into being and which sustained the culture until the genes were watered down.

Some of the quotes in the article could be said by whites with consciousness today. One man says "I always knew I was Gabrielino. But it wasn't cool to be Indian before. You were an outcast and wanted to hide that identity." "Hide that identity," sounds a lot like many neutral low consciousness aracial whites today who either don't have any sense of identity or who want to hide it lest they be treated with contempt as were the Indians when they expressed their identity in the past.

One wonders if it'll take a couple of hundred years, as it did with the Indians, and the almost full assimilation of white people, for many whites to understand that they have a right to their identity as white people and that this is something that has to be fought for, lest they go the way of the "lost" Indians of America.

It wasn't until the 1970's, when many Indians started becoming activists and demanding that they have the right to exist as distinct peoples that the larger society started noticing them and begrudgingly allowing them their rights.

That's the way it always is. A people has to demand the right to exist as a distinct people and it has to be strong enough in its in-group inclusiveness to stay separate and to maintain its own distinct culture and institutions or it will disappear into the larger society around it.

Whites were the absorbers and assimilators of the Indians and now it is whites who are in danger of being absorbed and assimilated. It's mostly a matter of the big fish eats the small fish, but there are some examples where the small fish has survived.

Consider the experience of the Jews who have, throughout most of their history, been in circumstances where they were the small fish surrounded by scores of big fish. How did they survive? Largely through the strong glue of a religious faith that was partly racial in nature by holding that a Jew was defined as a person born of a Jewish woman. Over the centuries, through all circumstances, this genetic requirement to being a Jew kept at least some of the primary genes of the group circulating within the group. Today, however, many Jews are bemoaning the increased assimilation of Jews through intermarriage with non-Jews, and while the arguments against intermarriage are often based, not on direct talk of genes, but on things such as maintaining Jewish "traditions," one of these traditions, remember, is the just mentioned Jewish Law that a Jew is defined as the child of a Jewish mother. So, it comes round robin back to genes even if it is not PC to talk of genes. As you may also know, Judaism is not a proselytizing faith, and does not seek converts because, after all, if one is not born of a Jewish mother then one lacks the traditional requirement of being a Jew. And, while it is possible for non-Jews to convert to some so-called modern branches of Judaism this is still relatively rare.

Among non-Jewish whites there is very little glue holding them together so that they become a distinct people. The Mormons were on the road to becoming a distinct people, but then they had a convenient PC revelation a few years ago that allowed non-whites to hold their priesthood. This was then accompanied by increased missionary activity among non-whites that is starting to blend the almost exclusively white Mormon church back into the non-white mass of humanity.

In past years, even though many whites didn't see themselves as a distinct people, there were still social pressures and laws to keep them from mating outside the general category "white," and this kept whites as a distinct people even though they weren't fully aware of what this meant. Today, however, these neutral aracial whites have often dropped previous resistance to mating outside the group and this further erodes even the weak group glue that once held them together.

Lacking any meaningful sense of identity; indeed, their identity is their bland lack of identity, many whites see no reason in even trying to maintain their non-identity.

Will we see groups of brown people in the future with names like Bush, doing then what many Indians are doing now; which is to say, will we pick up a newspaper in say 3009 and read about brown people trying to prove that they're really white people so the government will give them benefits?

Of course, when Indians or other non-whites speak of their identity or their culture and heritage, they are praised for their newly found consciousness, but when whites do it, they are often called "racists." That's just something that conscious whites are going to have to deal with until there is a critical mass of newly conscious whites in society who will demand that the haters stop their vile attacks on whites who know they're white.

Only when whites once again become activists and force, via the activism, others, including aracial whites, to see that whites have a right to exist as conscious whites will the hate towards whites end. And, only then will the anti-white bigots, who so easily dismiss any whites as racists and bigots just because these whites demand to have their identity, be shown for the true bigots and haters that they really are.

IS IT RACISM OR CONSCIOUSNESS?

Here's what someone told me about his experience in racial consciousness. Maybe his experience with rising consciousness is similar to that of other European-Americans in this nation. Maybe it isn't. You be the judge, but I'll bet that with some minor variations, many European-Americans have experienced the same thing.

In the small town where this guy was born and raised he saw no blacks, and no Hispanics. He did, however, once see a Chinese guy who owned a Chinese restaurant on the edge of town. The town was white. The streets were safe and that which passed for crime would go unnoticed in most major cities of this nation today. He never thought of myself as a European-American or even as a white person. He was just himself. He was concerned with himself and what he wanted and felt. He was an island unto himself. He had little knowledge of his living relatives and didn't care a whit who and what his ancestors were. He was, it can be guessed, something like a flatworm floating in a peaceful petri dish, and the peacefulness of the petri dish kept his consciousness low. There was no conflict and there was no struggle. Life was easy. His whole world was in the small insular town and in his feelings. If it was cold he moved to the heat. If it was hot he moved to the cool. That was life. He just existed in a low consciousness state.

His first experience with non-whites was when he went into the military. Some non-whites were good, some were bad. Some were industrious, some were lazy. Just like whites. No big deal. They were just white people with different paint jobs, he thought. They were just like white people and the only difference was in hue. He just minded his own business and didn't give any thought to the differences. He had a job to do and they had their jobs to do and they were all servicemen.

Then, he started experiencing hatred towards himself because he was white. Many of these experiences were subtle, but they were real. One of the first experiences came when a Jewish guy said to him, out of the blue, and for no reason that he could discern: "Jews are smarter. We control the banks." Before that, he didn't even know the guy was Jewish, and he wouldn't have given it a second thought if he had known. After that, he could never forget. He always wondered what motivated the Jew to even say such a thing. He had said nothing to bring it on. He was completely racially/ethnically/religiously neutral. For some reason just those few words which were said in a sort of pompous superior way started him noticing that people of different races/ethnicities just seemed to naturally act more like people of their race/ethnicity than like people of other races/ethnicities. That's when he started realizing that there was more to race/ethnicity than skin color.

He started reading, and one book led to another and it became ever clearer that people were really different from each other and that the reason was genes. People of this or that race/ethnicity were simply born different from people of different races/ethnicities.

"But so what?" he thought. If people hated him because he was white, that was their problem. The world was mostly white. At least that's what he thought from his childhood experience. Then he learned that his view of the world was wrong. In fact, he soon learned that the Earth was about 90% non-white. Whites were a small 10% minority on the planet. Suddenly, his petri dish existence was shaken. But, America was mostly white. So if non-white people hated white people that was just too bad because America—white America—was the strongest nation on Earth and the haters couldn't act out their hatred.

Then came massive non-white immigration to the U.S. and the hatred of the non-whites toward whites started being palpable. At the same time, certain elite whites were busy spreading propaganda calling whites who had some sense of their whiteness, haters, bigots and racists. "We're all just Americans," was and is one popular propaganda line. But of course this was only aimed at whites. Non-whites were encouraged to feel racial and ethnic pride.

And so it went. Finally America was no longer America. It had become post-American America. The nation had become a land that would be unrecognizable by the Founding Fathers. Now it seems that all the 90% non-white population of the planet is rushing to the American shores and America—which was formerly, although few say this—a New Europe, is becoming a Third World nation.

And as the nation devolved, there were still many whites out there in their petri dishes with no consciousness of who and what they were or that they actually came from something and did not spring whole and complete and alone out of nothing.

He saw these things and wanted to tell others about them. But, most whites seemed to be apathetic to their own genocide When he spoke of these things he was too easily dismissed as a racist, hater and bigot. At times he felt the way characters in some science fiction films seemed to feel when they saw that the aliens had landed and were taking over the world and turning everyone into zombies and no one would listen.

Still, he persisted, in his own small way, and here and there a few whites were snapped out of their propaganda induced almost hypnotic state and they too started crawling out of the petri dish. Many of these started to understand that they are not just plain "don't put a hyphen in my name" Americans, but that they are European-Americans with a heritage and a culture that go back hundreds of thousands of years and that long before this artificial nation "America" existed they were a distinct people different from all other peoples on this planet and that they now must once again reassert their essential natures and take their place as a fully conscious distinct people with their own genetic identity and self-determination and if they don't, that they face the prospect of extinction.

There's no end to this tale, because, as he said to me, "Much more must be done and millions of more whites need to be awakened before society reaches a critical mass of conscious white people capable of fighting off their extinction." "Hell," he said, "most white people don't even know they're a distinct people so how can they even fight the genocide? Remember from history about the vast flocks of the now extinct Carrier Pigeons? I like to imagine them as though they were intelligent but that they had as low consciousness as many whites in the world today. Not seeing themselves as being different from other breeds of pigeons, the Carrier Pigeons could not see the pattern of their extinction and could not defend themselves against the unseen genocidists. 'Why, we're all just pigeons. We're all the same under the feather, so if some of us are being killed off, it doesn't matter because there are still plenty of pigeons,' might have been the argument of a low consciousness Carrier Pigeon.

I sometimes wonder if white people will cease to exist simply because so many fail to even understand that they are different from other peoples and if they lose the differences through intermarrying that they will no longer exist? Will they go the way of the Carrier Pigeons?"

RECLAIMING "THEIR" HERITAGE

The Los Angeles Times constantly gives inadvertent illustrations about the confusion among some people in this nation over identity.

In one story some time ago about Korean children who were adopted by white families, we read how the Koreans were trying to claim their Korean heritage.

In brief, it seems that more than a few apparently aracial whites adopted a bunch of Korean kids 30 or 40 years ago much as the forbears of these whites had adopted American Indian kids in previous generations. It was just more of the unspoken belief among aracial whites that holds that all people are really white people inside different color skins and they only need to be around white people to let the inner whiteness come out. Don't accuse these whites of having any sense of identity or positive self-esteem about their whiteness. If they had any of these evil "racist" thoughts they would have adopted white kids.

Unfortunately for the white "parents," as the little Korean kids started growing up, they started realizing that they were different. In the article, we read how many of these Koreans experienced "identity crisises," had feelings of being "isolated and alienated," and lacked a "sense of belonging." What? You mean they didn't suffer from the white disease of being identyless drones and didn't learn to say "don't put no hyphens in my name, sonny, I'm just a plain American"? Genes actually had something to do with them being different? Huh? Koreans raised by whites were still Koreans? Go figure.

Many of these Koreans soon realized that their new mothers and fathers didn't look like them, and presumably they didn't think the same or even smell the same. How could that be? Do you mean they were a different race? Oh, noooooo. Why, why, it sounds like racism. Hey, wait a minute. These are non-whites so this can't be racism.

Well, this being the age of white dopes, many of the white "parents" of these Koreans are "sensitive" to the ethnic yearnings of the Koreans and are saying that the Koreans need to have Korean connections so they can have a strong ethnic identity and positive self esteem. How utterly white of these identyless "parents" to say such things. Of course, if they had white children themselves, some of these parents would probably be trying to deny their white kids any sense of identity because that would be "racism."

One Korean man who is now in his forties who was raised by whites said "All the things that made me an oddball [in America], I realized were my Korean traits. People used to say, 'What's the matter, why don't you smile?' Koreans aren't supposed to walk around like an idiot, smiling, I just fit right in, in Korea." What? Genetic smiles and facial expressions? Of course that's not racist when said by a non-white, but let a white say something like that and there would be the usual cries of racism.

Turn now from this article on Koreans finding their heritage to another article in the same paper about a "rude awakening on racism." In this article we learn how a black minister suddenly awoke to the evils of white racism when he learned that a white minister he had been associated with for years had told his (the white minister's) daughter not to date blacks."

Well, golly, the black minister was "dumbstruck" and upset about such overt racism. And to think he thought this white minister was his friend. How dare a WHITE actually care about his heritage and try to instill a "strong ethnic identity and positive self-esteem" in his daughter. Actually, the black minister didn't say those words in quotation marks in the second sentence above, that quote is from the earlier article on Koreans mentioned at the start of this column. Such an attitude was tacitly praised by the newspaper when it appeared in connection with Koreans but damned when applied to whites. Surprised?

It bears repeating until no white person can forget it and until no white person accepts it: What's praised in non-whites is condemned in whites. Of course whites with a sense of consciousness already know that. If more whites were more conscious about how and what they are, they'd see the double standard coming from major newspapers and elites in our society concerning race.

Koreans, we are told, raised to be aracial by aracial whites feel: "alienated, isolated, lack a sense of belonging, lack a strong ethnic identity and positive self-esteem." Guess what? Whites raised by aracial whites also feel: "alienated, isolated, lack a sense of belonging, lack a strong ethnic identity and positive self-esteem." This may be one of the reasons that we're seeing so many young whites striking out at society these days. They feel alienated. Their parents are often brain pithed aracials who lack any sense of identity themselves.

And what of the black minister mentioned above? Why, he's given up his alleged Uncle Tom ways (some blacks had previously considered him an Uncle Tom for his association with whites) and is now accepted back into the black community where he does such unracist things as supporting black causes.

This talk of Korean identity and black identity leads to the question: Is white identity coming? You bet. Times are changing, and whites are starting to emerge from the sleep of the past 40 years and are starting to realize that they are repressed and oppressed by a Blender establishment that has been keeping them brow beaten and in an intellectual prison ringed all about not with razor wire but with hate terms such as "racist, bigot, hater, prejudiced."

More and more whites, when they're called hate terms these days aren't retreating into a corner and aren't trying to prove that some of their best friends are.... Instead, they're mocking the white haters and showing them up for the bigots that they are, and more and more whites are finding a common sense of identity and community with their fellow whites.

It may not yet be a common expression among whites, but can "OURSELVES ALONE" be far off as a unifying slogan among whites who suddenly realize that they're a small 10% of humanity on this planet and that the 90% that is non-white doesn't like them very much even when the whites pander to the non-whites?

BRAINWASHING OF EUROPEAN-AMERICANS

BRAINWASH—to indoctrinate so intensively and thoroughly as to effect a radical transformation of beliefs and mental attitudes.

Apparently some European-Americans have been immune to the Pavlovian conditioning that exists in our public schools and in our society in general these days, and actually still have some sense of ethnic consciousness.

Unfortunately, some who have, for whatever reason, not been zombified by the conditioning often seem to be frustrated by the corrupt system that keeps them repressed, and they strike out in illegal ways rather than channeling their consciousness into positive legal efforts that help their people overcome the hidden repression, oppression and suppression that European-Americans face in America today on a daily basis and whose aim seems to be a final solution calculated to rid the world of white people (or at least, in the short term, white people who know they're white people).

In the Midwest, four men who burned a cross in front of a black family's house were ordered into a brainwashing program (euphemistically called "sensitivity training" by the court—considered by some to be part of the corrupt anti European-American establishment) where attempts will be made to reconstruct them through the watching of films such as "Schindler's List" and "Amistad," as well as having them participate in some sort of reeducation camp complete with group hug fests (euphemistically called "a special college program on cultural and social diversity"), where, no doubt, these four men will eventually be "welcomed back into humanity," with hugs and tears all around if and when the brainwashing is effective.

There was no mention in the news as to whether they'll also be subjected to sleep, food and water deprivation and other tools of brainwashing to break down their personalities so they can be remolded as the establishment desires. One suspects, however, that the establishment prefers more subtle techniques such as first setting up non-whites as boogey man like caricatures only to easily knock them down by showing these four men that "gee, they're people, just like us." No kidding. Of course they are. To think otherwise, is a mistake that isn't caused by so-called "racism" but by ignorance.

What, if anything, are we to make of the fact that the judge in this case, a guy with a Jewish sounding surname, sentenced these four European-Americans to watch films about the Jewish Holocaust and about Slavery (whites are the bad guys in both films, of course) made by another guy with a Jewish surname? Do the judge and film maker share anything in common that might be different from the four men that were sentenced? Might one reasonably suspect some type of inborn cultural bias against these four men? You be the judge.

One suspects that these four men are really being punished for their thoughts while the physical act of burning the cross is being used as a rationale to justify the punishment. If this isn't the case, then why are they being sentenced to what might be called thought modification?

The judge said that his first reaction was to lock the four men up and throw the key away, (Huh? It may have been an attempt at intimidation, but there was no attempt to physically harm anyone and no one was hurt) but that because the men showed remorse and a willingness to be rehabilitated (read, undergo brainwashing), the sentence would be lighter.

After the brainwashing is completed, we might even see one or more of these men showing up on TV shows where they'll confess their old evil ways and tell how they had been led astray by "racists" and how they've now come to see the light. (Cut to close ups of non-whites in the audience with tears streaming down their cheeks while beaming big smiles).

Now, the terrorizing of anyone of any race requires punishment, and the facts published in this case seem to indicate that such terrorizing was going on and that punishment is deserved. No good decent person would argue otherwise. However, the type of brainwashing that seems to be going on here, is not proper punishment. Sure, these guys should be told that it's not acceptable to intimidate others as they did and they should be given some sort of sensitivity training, but such sensitivity training should be balanced.

What is more troubling than this case, however, is other instances where European-Americans have been prosecuted for burning crosses and engaging in other exercises of their free speech rights on their own properties and often far away from homeowners of any race, but are then arrested and prosecuted.

What happens is that those who hate European-Americans often shift and blur lines in many of these instances so that the legal expression of ideas becomes associated, in the public mind, with illegal harassment. Burning a cross or even a pile of leaves on one's own property when not intended to harass others should be legal under the First Amendment. Burning a cross or a pile of old tires on someone else's property with the intent to harass them is illegal.

A distinction must be made, otherwise we begin to lose our free expression rights in this country.

Because so many European-Americans are becoming frustrated with the corrupt system in this country that keeps them down, and because so many are striking out in illegal ways, it's important for all good decent European-Americans with any sense of self and group worth and with even a modicum of consciousness to reach out to those who are alienated and help them channel their energies into law abiding activities to help their people. Otherwise, many will be sent to the reeducation camps only to return as spiritless drones.

The brainwashing should be resisted by all good decent people, but at the same time, it must be understood that until European-Americans can openly express ethnic pride, that there will be those who will become frustrated and strike out in illegal ways.

The answer is not reeducation camps, but a transformation of our society to allow European-Americans their full rights to self-definition, self-determination and survival as a distinct people.

MELLOW YELLOW

Proponents of the "we're all one race," swill took another hit recently when scientists revealed that bananas share about 50% of the DNA of humans (I kid you not). This is 10% more than what we share with earthworms. Add this information to the previous revelation that humans and chimps are 98.4% the same genetically, and you begin to see the problem for the we're all one race crowd—our present ignorant flat worlders. The reason this is a hit for the all one race crackpots is because it is just a further indication that nature works with minor changes to make major differences. In fact, there are no "tiny" changes in nature at the DNA level of existence. Just a minor change here or there makes a totally different animal or plant.

Sure, everything in existence is the same at some level. After all, we've all risen from the same inert chemicals that exist in the universe, and all of us on earth have come into existence as living things by the same basic processes. But, in nature, it is not the things in common that living things have with one another that are most important, but the things not in common. This is so, because nature is about constant change and this constant change enables both evolution and devolution. Some PC types say that we should just overlook the differences between the human races, and that this is the way for everyone to get along. This is baloney. It is counter to evolution and nature and the logical conclusion of this is to have humans become a lumpen genetically conforming Tan Everyman clustered under the center of the bell curve in skin color, racial characteristics, I.Q. and all other factors. Such thinking is a recipe for mediocrity and a slowing down of evolution.

What we should be doing is appreciating the uniqueness of different human types and emphasizing our differences so that the species will evolve. It is going to be the different ones, the ones on the extreme legs of the bell curve, who will lead to a higher type, not those clustered in the middle in all genetic characteristics. Those in the middle are the compost heap of the species from which new forms arise. Unfortunately for human evolution, humans, at the very time that so many are saying they love diversity, seem to be doing everything possible to cause all humans to conform to the Tan Everyman type. Of course, the reality is that most people praising diversity don't really want diversity at all. What they are really doing (whether they are conscious of this or not) is trying to get rid of white people, and they're using diversity talk to make whites more accepting of mating with non-whites and thus moving white family lines away from the white norm.

What do we mean by evolution and devolution? Evolution is the upward movement of something. Devolution is a downward movement. What do we mean by upward and downward? Upward is to higher consciousness. Downward is to lower consciousness. What do we mean by higher consciousness? Higher consciousness is a vague term that encompasses various products of the mind including higher intelligence, higher awareness, a greater sense of Being, and more "life." Lower consciousness is the opposite. It is lower intelligence, lower awareness, a lower sense of Being and less "life." Consciousness is on a scale. One can, for example, say that a rock lacks most consciousness (however, this is not quite true, because even a rock has atoms that are moving, and movement indicates that something is not completely "dead.").

As far as we know, humans are the most conscious animals. If there is a God, then God, if assumed to be as He is thought to be in many religions, is the most conscious entity in the universe. His is a consciousness that exists without a body and brain as we know them. Such a Supreme Being is probably here and there all at the same time and He is probably within and without everything in existence. Would be so far off to postulate that He is a disembodied spirit or some sort of sub atomic particle or group of such particles or a wave or a force or an energy that is whole and complete in each part of his being no matter where this is found, which is everywhere and that He knows everything about everything all at the same time because He is there all at the same time? If we assume that God is within everything that exists, then we are left to conclude that God within a rock is limited to "rockness," and God within a tree is limited to "treeness." If not, then rocks and trees would probably have powers beyond what they do have. If God is the ultimate consciousness, and experiences things, at least partly, through that which he is within, one can probably tentatively conclude that God may also want to be in something that experiences more than, say, a rock. Might we not also conclude then, at least as a theory, that God wants to evolve matter so that God in matter will have more consciousness? If we do accept this notion, then we are led to believe that God probably wants to evolve humans so that humans will better know Him and so He will experience more. Yes, this suddenly begins to sound like what is taught in various religions, but not always in similar words. And while this argues for the unity of everything in existence, it also argues for the evolution of everything in existence so that something in existence will evolve to be the highest possible vessel for God.

Leading the way for being the highest possible vessel for God appears to be the human species, but it is far from that point, and it will never reach that point unless parts of it can evolve ever higher. This means that some human types will become extinct and disappear from the face of the earth, and some types will move upward. Of course, it could go the other way. The much ballyhooed human "free will" and the ability to choose between right and wrong and resist temptation play a part in all of this, because right and wrong are far more than things such as whether one should steal or not steal or lie or not lie. Real right and wrong and real resisting temptation relate to mating choices. If we mate properly we can move higher. If we mate improperly we can move lower. We have the choice to do either. Those who hate us, and dare we say it, who also hate God, want us to devolve and they try to deceive us with lies so that we will fall into improper mating and other practices that reduce our numbers, and destroy our genes.

Unfortunately, most humans lack the consciousness to see much of this and many are blinded by the evil doers who want us destroyed. These are the ones who are doing things that lead to devolution. They deny the differences between different human types and, in so denying, they open the possibility that they will devolve their lines. As they devolve, they may eventually deny the differences between chimps and humans. If they keep going in that direction they will eventually lack the consciousness to know the difference between themselves and bananas.

ANOTHER SWASTIKA, ANOTHER RELIGION

Symbols are important for a number of reasons. They can represent a belief system, a nation, a people. They can rally the faithful and inspire them and they can intimidate one's enemies. Some believe that certain symbols are much more than mere symbols and that they forge a link with unseen forces in the universe. But more of this a little later.

Several years ago a toy model company which was known for its detailed and accurate models of various nation's war planes, and other military equipment was forced by some haters of all things European-American to remove the Swastika from various Nazi era models.

Then a major California daily newspaper figured it had found some secret Nazis in the community when some local woman got hysterical and almost got the vapors when she noticed a Swastika in front of a building that she had passed. There was much breast beating and teeth gnashing and the newspaper was soon full of the typical letters from the neurotic cat ladies (sans cats) who wanted to hold huggy kissy candle light vigils and the like. Then it was revealed that the Swastika was in front of a Buddhist religious group's headquarters. Oops. The ignorant complainers had been so blinded by their hatred, their stupidity and their conditioning that their jerking knees had over ridden any higher brain functions that they might have been capable of having.

The Swastika is used by Buddhists as a sacred symbol. Why is this relevant now? Well, with the many news reports concerning the repression of the Falun Dafa sect in China, the Swastika is now back in the public's view. As you may know, the Falun Dafa apparently has many thousands of believers who regularly meet in parks and open spaces in China to perform their exercises which they believe will harmonize them with the universe. One of the first images on their Website (at least as this is written) is a Swastika.

It's not just the Buddhists who use the Swastika as a sacred symbol. There are apparently some European-Americans who believe that the Swastika truly is a religious symbol that connects them with the power(s) of the universe in a sort of sympathetic magical way. Let me digress for a moment to explain this term "sympathetic magic" a little.

The term means that one can make an image of something real that may be far away and that there will be an invisible link between the image and the real thing, and that one can manipulate the real thing by the use of the image. Don't laugh. What do you think you're doing when you pray? You're just trying to influence your vision of God by asking Him to do or not do something. Your prayerful words are an attempt to manipulate the world around you.

Scholars over the years have given various opinions as to the "meaning" of the Swastika. Some hold that it is a sun symbol and represents the sun traveling across the heavens each day. Others say that it is a good luck symbol (there's that sympathetic magic again). The European-American's I mentioned in the paragraph above, believe the Swastika is a representation of the power of the universe and is in effect the "face of God," and the engine of creation and destruction. They explain that the Swastika can be seen everyplace we look. It's in the skies in the form of spiral galaxies, it's in our kitchen sinks when the water drains out, it's in the way trees grow, it's in our DNA, it's in every hurricane and tornado. To these people, the Swastika is the most active form of the Spiral that is the orderer of the universe. It is the mechanism of self-sorting and self-segregating. It is what makes everything work in the entire universe from the tiniest unseen things to the largest things.

They further believe that the Swastika can help them "receive" various "God waves" the way the parts of a radio help us pick up ever present radio waves, and that it activates something that they call "essence" which they apparently believe they received as part of their genetic heritage.

These people also believe that there really is a battle going on in the universe between good and evil, light and dark, and that they represent all that is good and light and those who oppose the Swastika are evil. Although this sounds a little like certain Christian theology, these people are not Christians and believe that Christianity is a force of the dark. They explain that in their belief system the universe was all dark at the beginning and that God awoke and fed off the darkness to come into our universe. They see this as being a tiny point of light starting in the darkness which began to vibrate and jump up and down and spin on a central axis. As the tiny point of light spun it put out arms as it gathered matter to itself and appeared as a Swastika (with more rounded arms than the Swastika we normally see). In this belief system, the center of the Swastika is something like a black hole pulling all that is near it into itself and using what is pulled in to create a new reality. In this regard, they see the Swastika as something like a Cornucopia (or horn of plenty), the mythical horn from which anything and everything flowed forth into the universe.

These people believe that God, although He is not the light itself, is present in the light. They sometimes say that the light is God's steed. They also believe that one can never see God directly, but that He can be seen in the Swastika as He wishes to be seen. They also believe that God wants believers to use the Swastika as a sacred symbol and that this serves the additional purpose of helping to identify those who hate God when such people express their hatred about the Swastika.

Another peculiar aspect of this belief system is that believers sometimes refer to God as the Wind Out of the Far Places, and apparently this is the reason that they apparently practice their religious rites in the out of doors and especially during storms which they also consider holy. In a way, it appears that this belief system, is something of a nature religion, but with some additional elements, including a belief that genes are important to knowing God, and if you don't have the right genes, you can never know God, just as if you don't have the right parts in your radio you'll never be able to pick up radio waves.

So, the next time you see a Swastika, don't jump to the conclusion that it necessarily represents a strictly political view. It may represent Buddhists, or Falun Dafa or even the folks mentioned above.

LIFE'S LOSERS?

It has become fashionable and common among certain white elites—even among some who call themselves conservatives—to refer to non-elite whites in a variety of disparaging and insulting terms. "Life's losers, trailer trash, white trash, bubbas, low life scum, red necks, bigots, racists," are a few of these hateful terms.

Just who are these "losers" that the white elites like to insult, apparently in the belief that these so-called losers lack the intelligence and means to fight back? Many are military veterans who thought it their duty to serve their country instead of scamming a deferment. And while these veterans were going to jungles and deserts, the white elites were going to places like Harvard and Yale, and getting a leg up on life.

And while these veterans were doing their duty, Opportunity often went looking for candidates. When Opportunity knocked on the doors of the then serving servicemen and women, they often weren't home to answer the door. They were in uniform. So, Opportunity went to other doors and he found the draft dodgers and the shirkers, and they gladly opened their doors.

Meanwhile, the young men and women in the military were losing more than just a few years of their lives, because most had gone into the service at a crucial time for emotional and psychological development of their personalities. They were often young, and their minds were molded by the military in many subtle and not so subtle ways that sometimes made them less open to certain opportunities once they left the service.

When these service people came home, they were often disrespected and treated like dirt. These "losers" were now too old—if not in actual years, then in emotional years—to easily fit into a college setting or to take jobs as mail clerks at the bottom of the rung of major corporations. While in the service they had often been in life and death situations and now they were treated as though they should be box boys and box girls.

In fact, these service people had missed several rungs of the ladder to success while they were in the service. Furthermore, they often didn't have the network of civilian friends that they might have developed had they not gone into the service. They could feel their difference—their alienation and cosmic aloneness—and so could those in their old home towns. They were God's loners. They were forever changed.

These "losers" were and are the salt of the Earth. For the most part they're honest and direct. They are mostly people of their word, and they mostly avoid scams and flim flammery in making a living. They want to do honest work for honest pay and to be left alone to raise their families—as they want—in peace and happiness.

They want better for their children than they themselves have, and they work hard to accomplish this. They are mostly good and decent people.

But what do they constantly hear from the white elites? They hear that they are life's losers and white trash. They hear lectures that they must give up their kids' college seats to less qualified students because of skin color. They hear that they can't defend themselves from violent street criminals. They hear that they must give up their place in the job line because of their white skin, and that they are "evil" and "racist" if they resist. They hear that they must let illegal immigrants take their jobs. They hear that they are stupid if they don't want the white elites to move factories to foreign lands. They hear white elite politicians lying to them on a daily basis.

And while these "losers" are living good honest lives, they read or hear about white elites who have cheated their way to the top, often by hurting little people of all races. And as time goes by, the "losers" start to awaken to the fact that are not like the white elites at all. They are a people made different by the thousands of little experiences that they have had in their lives that the white elites have not had. They start to realize that they are a people alone.

And when they come to this realization—this grand awakening—they suddenly are freed to start acting in their own best interests with no false illusions that they can turn that lawn mowing business into a billion dollar industry as some white elites keep telling them, in an attempt to keep them stupid and happy. "Why, just work hard," comes the voice of a multi-millionaire radio talk show host, "and you can accomplish as much as I have." Sure. That's the way this guy got to the top; by working hard at a lawn mowing business. Who does he think he's kidding? And these "losers" start to throw over the false ideas of the nature of man that the white elites have tried to stuff down their throats.

When these" losers" awaken and finally realize who and what they are and stop apologizing for it, and when they stop letting the white elites browbeat them and make them feel worthless, they come to the realization that they do have worth. They are not life's losers at all, and that when acting together with those like them that they have far more power than the few white elites who have called them names.

Still, there are some who don't understand this, and they try hard to not be what it is that the white elites call them, and they never realize that they must look out for their own, and let other groups look out for their own as well. It is a sad spectacle to see some of these people try to forge alliances with people unlike themselves, because these alliances ultimately fail as the group will of these "losers" is diluted by the will of others.

It is time that these non-elite whites took their places in the affairs of this world boldly and with no apologies. It is time that these non-elite whites asserted their peoplehood and their rights. It is time that these non-elite whites stopped running every time they are called names, but give measure for measure.

But most of all, it is time that these non-elite whites started organizing so that their voices can be heard and so that they can't be easily dismissed by the white elites.

Life's losers? Don't you believe it! These are life's winners, and if they have faults it is that they are too forgiving of insults to themselves and they turn their cheeks too many times and they are too tolerant of those who would destroy them; they are too patient; and they are too unaware that they are a distinct people with God given rights that they must assert and fight for, or they will be trampled both by white elites and by non-whites.

These "losers" are the people who built this nation and who will take it back if they are able to come out of the darkness of their souls put there by the white elites; and to boldly assert their right to be themselves—as they themselves define themselves.

WHACKO BLENDERS PUSH GENOCIDE

Genocide—"the systematic killing of, or a program of action intended to destroy, a whole national or ethnic group.

"Blenders" is the name I've given to what others call multiculturalism or multiracialism or the One World Order. I chose this word because I believe it more correctly characterizes what those who push the concept have in mind. "Multiculturalism" and "multiracialism" sound as though there are a bunch of different cultures and races in a society that are to be kept separate and distinct—a series of China Towns and Little Saigons, for example. "One World Order" seems to have taken on meanings of an economic or political fusion of all the different nations of the Earth—a grand version of NAFTA, perhaps. The word "Blenders," on the other hand, indicates that those pushing multiculturalism, multiracialism and the One World Order are really trying to blend all races, nations and religions into what I've called the Tan Everyman—the universal human model.

Much of the mainstream media pushes Blending the way cigarette companies push their products. In fact, when future historians write of this epoch they will no doubt discuss what is probably the most massive propaganda campaign in history as the Blenders work 24 hours a day to make self-genocide acceptable to distinct peoples around the world.

The Los Angeles Times gave an example a few years ago of what the Blenders are doing to convince people to commit genocide on themselves. In a gushy front page story "Learning to Look Beyond Race," we see smiling people of different races dancing with each other in the city of Walnut, located in Los Angeles County.

In the story, readers are told that "Walnut's young people, seeing friends rather than skin color, may represent America's future." We are then told that Walnut "went from predominantly white to two-thirds Asian, black or Latino in a generation," and is now "among the most diverse (cities) in America." And a little further in the story we read "Today, members of Walnut's white old guard find themselves proud grandparents of children of partly Asian, Latino and black heritage." Gush, gush.

We also read that back when the population was changing, a white woman started a 50 member Anglo-American Club as an alternative to the many ethnic clubs that were forming in the city and how one black woman who was convinced that "the club was a cover for a racist, whites-only group, not a bastion of ethnic pride, tried to force the issue by asking if she would be eligible to join. An Anglo member replied that 'she didn't see why on Earth' the woman would want to—and word of the exchange spread all over town." Soon, many white people in the town "express(ed) their outrage," over the comments by the white woman and the club fizzled." Gush, gush. The article went on and on in that vein. It was all about racial blending

Then, in the same edition there was another article: "What Religious Diversity Sounds Like," which was about various Christian churches and other religious groups opening the doors of their religious buildings to music of various faiths during a festival.

Also in the same edition is a photo of black opera soprano in a semi-romantic clutch with a white tenor s the two prepare to perform "Samson et Dalila," at L.A. Opera's premiere.

Examples of Blending propaganda and psychological conditioning could go on and on, and it's not just the Los Angeles Times that is pushing this concept. Check your own newspapers where you live and you'll see the same thing, or go to the movies or watch TV. Blending is being pushed in thousands of ways the way breakfast cereal is pushed.

If you think such propaganda doesn't work, then you're not aware of how easy it is to persuade people to do things via such propaganda. The entire advertising industry is based on being able to convince you to buy things with words and images that seep into your subconscious mind. All things good are associated with the product, say, cigarettes, and your subconscious mind then makes you buy a pack based on the image. You may deny that's what motivated you to make your purchase and you may be honest in your denial—at least in a conscious sense—but your subconscious has told you that you want to be like those beautiful and slim (if you're a woman) or cool or with it, or ruggedly handsome (if you're a man) people smiling on that billboard and smoking a particular brand of cigarette.

But, the real issue about Blending vs. non-Blending is one about the nature of man, the universe and, yes, God. If one believes that there are no real and meaningful differences between the races of man (as the Blenders push) then

Blending isn't really even blending at all, it's just the normal interaction between people. If, however, one believes that there are very real and meaningful differences between the races and that God demands separation, then blending is evil. Or, if God is left out of the equation, but one believes that evolution demands that the races remain separate so that nature can improve the species by causing differences to develop among different populations, then bending is bad, since blending will erase all differences and make all humans be of one type.

How does anyone know what is right and wrong in all of this? Well, those who follow the literal word of the Christian God believe that humans have free will and they are told by God to make a choice in life between good and evil. Both options are open to them and they can do good or they can do evil. Those who believe this way know that just because someone can do something doesn't make it right.

However, few of these people, thanks to the mind bending propaganda they've been exposed to, understand that the same principle applies to mating. Few would be un-PC enough these days to say that just because people of one group can mate with people of another group doesn't make it right. Thus are many people led to evil, according to those who believe that mating outside the race is evil.

In the general Christian view, God knows that His creation is weak and must have guidance to avoid evil. For that reason, He has given His law and demands to man and man is to be guided in his choices in life by God's word. Herein, lies another problem because the so-called Word of God—the Christian Bible—has been given so many different translations and interpretations that people are confused and can find just about anything they want by sentence and church shopping. The answer to this dilemma, if one must be a Christian, is to find a church that relies on older non-Blender translations of the Bible and other religious books. What did God really demand? You need to find that out, and you won't find that in Blender churches which change to suit the changing fashions of every age. What about different religions? If God supposedly gave His truths to various religions, why do the modern adherents believe that they can modify these truths to be more acceptable to other religions? Is God real or is He just an invention of humans to justify compelling people to act in certain ways? If He's real, and if He said something back in history that was supposed to be for all times, then chances are He meant it for all times.

Suppose you're not religiously disposed, how can you know what is right and wrong? You need to look at true science and learn about genetics, evolution and other matters about how nature works to improve a species. Why are there different races to begin with? Are the different races only different in "minor" things such as skin colors or are there many more differences, and are these differences important? What does evolution really mean for man? What would a higher evolved human look and act like? Will such a being be able to run faster and have sharper teeth or will he have more of those things of the brain that have now put him above all other animals? Should humans breed for brute strength or stronger minds? If you answer, both, then you fail to see the engineering problem that exists in making a human. If you give him more of this you have to short him out on something else in order to fit him into a viable package. Nature, or even God, if you prefer, must work with natural laws in creating everything.

On another level; no matter what race they belong to, people should be insulted that they're being manipulated by the Blenders into being consumers of the genocide of their particular genotypes. Those who are in the most danger of immediate genocide are white people. This is so because white people are a very tiny 10% minority on this planet. Fully 90% of all humans are non-white. Blacks are also in danger of disappearing from the face of the Earth with such Blending, but that's a problem that blacks, themselves, will have to address. To each his own.

Furthermore, if you plot out human populations based on, say, skin color, you'll find that most cluster in the center while the whitest and the blackest are out on the legs of what will be a standard Bell Curve. It is always the extremes—the few—that are in the most danger of being destroyed. And, the extremes of race are in danger of genocide via blending.

CAN YOU FIND THE HATE CRIMES?

"White Man is beaten, dragged by American Indians." The Indians are arrested and everyone in sight tries to prove that this isn't a hate crime, but is attributable to alcohol, or drugs.

"Black Man is beaten, dragged by Whites." The whites are arrested and everyone in sight tries to prove that this is a hate crime and is not attributable to alcohol nor drugs.

After a traffic accident, a black driver calls a white driver "Stupid Honky," and the white driver then calls the black driver "Stupid Nigger." The white driver is arrested and prosecuted for a hate crime. The black driver is not.

If your answer, in each case, is that the white, even in the first instance above, will in some way be blamed as a hate criminal or at least be considered to be at fault, then give yourself a star for having some understanding of the way it is in post-American America where whites are presumed culpable in some way just because of the color of their skin.

In the case of the white man dragged and left for dead by Indians, there was very little press on the subject even though it actually happened South Dakota. The 21 year old white victim, who had been drinking with some Indian "pals," before they attacked him, was hardly in his hospital bed before the F.B.I. and federal prosecutors said it was too early to label the assault a hate crime.

Police said that the victim had been dragged around a field by a rope tied around his neck and he was kicked so hard in the face with steel-toe boots that he was almost unrecognizable. His left ear was apparently almost torn off and his right ear was badly damaged. There was no mention of whether he had been scalped.

No hate crime there. Nope. Nope. Can't find any signs of hate. Just a bunch of fun loving non-whites who chose to try to kill, not one of their other non-white drinking pals, but the only white guy among them.

Given the nature of this crime—and it's only one of many such crimes perpetrated by non-whites against whites—and what appears to be an attempt to do head stands to prove that it's not a hate crime, is it any wonder that many whites are getting disgusted and fed up with the way they're being discriminated against in this nation?

Is it any wonder that some whites strike out at those they perceive to be the oppressors of whites? And, isn't it interesting that the ruling class elite media, when some white does strike out, run a constant stream of PR level stories about "hate," and "senseless hateful acts by whites" that the ruling class elite media seems hard pressed to understand? "Golly, we don't know what set this or that white person off, it's all a big surprise why this white did this horrible act." It should be no surprise at all. Anytime a society has a double standard where it treats one group better than another, frustration builds and those individuals in the group that isn't treated as well may sometimes strike out at others.

So what's the answer? Treat all citizens the same. Give no special favors to any groups. If you define this or that as hate when whites do it, then similar things done by non-whites should also be defined as hate. When our society truly treats whites no differently than non-whites then the level of frustration will drop among whites.

UGLY DUCKLING OR SWAN?

We've all heard the story about the Ugly Duckling who didn't look anything like any of the ducks and who was ashamed over being different from all the other ducks. The ugly duckling experienced a serious identity crisis and wanted to be like the other ducks, and be accepted as a duck. However, nothing he could do could make him like the ducks. The problem was that he wasn't a duck at all, but a swan. His genes made him what he was and so long as he stayed with the ducks, he was an outcast. When he finally joined with other swans he found himself, and his identity. As a swan, he was perfect. As a duck he was always imperfect. It is not much different with people.

In America today, we often hear European-Americans complaining about various racially segregated organizations such as the Latino Business Association, the Asian Business Association, the Black Women's Association, the Black Miss America contest, the Black Police Officers' Association and many others. So far so good. Then these complainers often say something along the lines of "I don't care if one is black, white, brown or yellow, but why can't we all just be Americans?"

Why indeed?

The answer is because we're not just Americans. There is no "American" race or genotype. It is an artificial term used to describe different peoples who happen to live on this chunk of dirt. Common usage once held that an American was a white person, but today in what I call post-American America, the old usage is no longer valid. When this nation was founded, it was the European genotype that was the norm as an American. No rewriting of history can change that fact. Whether seen as good or bad, a European descended person living in America (or, white person, if you prefer) was considered to be an "American." Sure, there were other peoples living here, but they were in such a small minority that they always had hyphens, or were simply identified as, say,

Chinese, or some similar national term to distinguish who they really were from the standard American. Thus, if one were writing to someone, that "I met an American today," the picture conjured up, in the mind of the reader, would automatically be one of a white person. Suppose the person being written about was black? Saying, "I met a black-American," or "I met a black from America," would give a realistic description of the person. Hyphens or some other means are needed to correctly identify someone, if a correct description is to be given.

Today, with the massive influx of mostly brown mestizo Latin Americans to this nation and with the push by the Blenders (those who want all races to be mixed together into one new artificial Tan Everyman race) to give them citizenship once they've been able to break our laws long enough and remain in this country for a certain period of time, the term "American" becomes even less viable to describe anyone who lives in this nation.

The issue is one of meaningful identity.

The European-Americans who eschew hyphens for themselves and who ask others to also not use them, fail to understand the reality of genotypes (or, its synonym, races). Part of this lack of understanding is caused by a subconscious belief that all people are really white people under different color skins, and that the white model for humanity is the basic model. In this view, all peoples would be as "polite and good" and all those other positive things that these low consciousness whites often attribute to whites, if only those inner white people could be released from their dark skin prisons.

We'll often hear these low consciousness European-Americans puffing up their chests as they tell everyone that this or that person they know is "black," but by golly "he's just an American." Oh, really? Then why did the European-American first identify the person as black? What's going on here is that many such European-Americans have a subconscious sense of identity but it is unauthentic because, as written above, it sees all people as white people with different color paint jobs. Such an unauthentic belief robs non-white peoples of their natural identities and it also robs whites of theirs. It is a belief system that leads to the greatest alienation of all—alienation from what one truly is. It also leads to alienation from people like oneself because one in the grip of this false belief system fails to see people who are like oneself as actually like oneself while at the same time seeing people unlike oneself as like oneself.

In America today, the alienated ones are primarily white people. It is these white people—these European-Americans—who are drifting aimlessly through life with no sense of meaning or purpose and this meaningless and purposelessness is largely caused by their alienation from their true selves and from those like themselves. Instead of finding their authentic identity, they instead, seek to find their identity in ever more artificial things. Thus you'll find many European-Americans identifying with their favorite sport or sports team or their hobby or religion or their occupation, but almost never with their essential selves—that genetic complement that they were born with that is the most important identifier of all.

Such people are like the Ugly Duckling, trying to fit into a world of others who are unlike them and never understanding that they'll never fit in with these others because they are different as a result of their genes.

But, you may be saying that the Ugly Duckling analogy is backwards and that it's the non-white peoples who feel like the Ugly Ducklings in our society and that's why they seek to find their identity—once their consciousness reaches a certain level—in those organizations mentioned at the outset of this column. In this you're wrong, because the reality of our planet is that while whites may be in a majority in certain small areas, they account for only 10% of the human population on Earth.

If whites have a sense of being all alone on Earth, there's a reason for the feeling. They are alone. They're a strange people on a strange planet and their existence as a people is threatened by the 90% of humans who are unlike them and by those among them whose consciousness is so low that they fail to see that they are a distinct people. Instead of trying to blend into the rest of humanity, whites should be trying to distill themselves out so they can avoid the genocide that is their fate with such blending. Instead of trying to be like other peoples, whites should be understanding that they are a unique people with a right to exist as a unique people, and that their continued existence as a people requires that they raise their consciousness and understand that by wanting to continue to exist as they are, is not, as they are told by anti-white bigots, hatred.

Back to the non-white organizations mentioned above. The European-Americans who ask why there should be such organizations should be asking why there aren't white equivalents to these organizations and if the answer is because they'll be called the usual hate terms of "racists, bigots," etc. then they need to raise their consciousness and disregard the hate from the anti-white bigots.

It's time that whites had their own separate organizations to look out for white interests and it's time that whites had their consciousness raised and found their identity, meaning and purpose.

It's time whites started thinking of themselves as a people. It's time whites started knowing who is like them—who is OURSELVES, and who is not, and it's time whites started realizing that they're ALONE. OURSELVES ALONE!

CONFORM! NO PINK MONKEYS ALLOWED

An experiment in prejudice was once conducted using monkeys. A monkey was removed from a group of monkeys and was painted pink. It was then reintroduced into the group. The other monkeys then attacked the pink monkey. Presumably, the reason for the attack was that the pink monkey was different than the norm for the group. We can look at this experiment and postulate several theories as to the root causes and their reasons for the monkeys' behavior, but more interesting, perhaps, is the interpretation put on the behavior by humans, who will show their own prejudices in their opinions.

Those who push Blending are likely to say that the attack behavior was caused by an irrational hatred of the color of the now pink monkey. They'll then leave the explanation at that, with of course a few comments about human "racism" following the same example. They'll say, for example, that those humans who "hate" others because of a different color are as dumb as the monkeys. While this is a nice pat and standard answer, it fails to address the underlying reasons for such feelings of dislike.

These underlying reasons actually appear to be a survival reaction and nature's way of preserving the integrity of a particular type. Such behavior on the part of monkeys or man doesn't even need to reach the conscious level where the attackers form the thought, "I hate them." Instead, it appears to be part of the genetic program of each creature to want to survive as an individual. Such survival of the individual seems to be more likely when others like oneself also survive, and when the group is uncorrupted by those that are different. This is the real reason why healthy humans automatically try to preserve others like themselves.

Man, however, arrogantly believes that he is above nature and that he can override nature and is therefore not subject to nature's laws. And, of course, in many ways man can override nature, but the question becomes one of whether this is always desirable. Should man, for example, override his dislike of those different from him, so that he not only does not attack them, but mates with them? And if he does, what does this mean for the survival of his type of man?

The answer is that such overriding of nature in this instance leads to a conformity of genes all clustered under the basic bell curve. The extremes are bred out of the population and the members tend to all be much alike not only in appearance but in abilities or lack of abilities, as well.

So what's the problem with that? Just that such clustering not only leaves out the least desirable traits, but it also leaves out the most desirable ones as well. This means that such clustering in the middle of the bell curve leads to a population of mediocrity.

Instead of attacking and driving off the pink monkeys that arise in human populations, the Blenders would destroy them by mating with them and thus eliminating their differences from the population by swamping their genes with the common ones.

So, we're left with what at first seems like a paradox. Those creatures who dislike others because of their differences and thus chase them away, are actually helping these different ones survive and are actually contributing to evolution by isolating those that are different where these different ones may mate and actually spread their differences as part of a different group that, if successful, may eventually challenge the first group for dominance. On the other hand, those creatures who don't dislike others because of their differences or who overtook the differences and eventually mate with the different ones are acting in an anti-evolutionary manner because they are breeding away the differences and moving toward the norm.

So, what does this mean for humans? As I've written elsewhere, the Blenders have the belief that all humans should ignore differences and freely mate with one another. The ultimate result of this would of course be a bland conformity of human type clustered around the center of the Bell Curve. In terms of just one characteristic—skin color—this means that the blackest and the whitest would be destroyed and the basic human type would be what I've called the Tan Everyman. This Tan Everyman would be in the middle of all traits. He would have brown skin, black hair, brown eyes and in stature would be of medium height. In mental abilities he would also be in the middle.

It is in this last item; mental abilities, that the real problem with the Tan Everyman will be found, because to be average in mental abilities does not bode well for the advancement of the species. This is especially true because humans are the thinking animals on this planet. Our dominance of the planet isn't due to brute strength, or running ability, but because of our ability to think.

The world of the Tan Everyman won't be the utopia that those who are pushing the concept believe, but a world that demands conformity in all things. It'll be a world where everyone thinks alike or is made to think alike. It'll be a world where few new thoughts will be put forth lest one be marked as a non-conformist.

Indeed, are we not seeing much of this type of conformity already overtaking us? We see such conformity first in social norms that are demanded of a population. In China today, those who practice certain forms of Christianity are arrested because their form of the religion is not "state approved." In the U.S. we see similar types of things. The folks at Waco didn't practice a state approved form of religion. Neither did Randy Weaver and his family. Take a look around at all the haters who attack people who follow Christian Identity or the Church of the Creator or similar faiths. Take a look at the hate that is thrown at many people on the right in politics because of their beliefs.

The message being sent by haters is conform or die. Be like the norm or you'll be attacked.

NOT QUITE YOURSELF ANYMORE, MON?

A familiar plot in science fiction films involves a human population in a town being taken over one by one by aliens who in one manner or another get inside the humans and transform them; usually into monotone zombies (well, after all, the film makers have to indicate that something is different about the former humans). These zombified humans then go on to try to take over more humans for their alien inner masters.

Well, I'm here to tell, you dear friends, THEY'RE HERE! THEY'RE HERE! and they're zombifying people all around you.

Perhaps a good example of this zombifying is illustrated by a small community in Jamaica. Most of the people in the community, as is the case all over Jamaica, are black. However, if you visit the area, don't be surprised if you're approached by a black man who may say something like this to you: "Welcome, mon. Can you spare some change for a fellow white man—a German, even?" Your reply may be, "Huh? I don't get it. You're black not white."

"No, mon. I be German. I swear to you. Say, would you like to buy some ganja, mon? Looka here mon, here's a photograph of me Great Grand Pa."

You look at the photo offered to you and you see the picture of a white man who could well be German.

"That's your Grandfather?" you ask.

"Yea, mon, that be him. He come to Jamaica wit' 500 other Germans back in the 1800's. Whole town was a full of dem white Germans. No blacks."

"So what happened?" you ask.

"They marry Jamaicans, mon. They lose that horrible white skin, that blonde hair and them blue eyes. They become Jamaicans, mon. Most all da black folk in the town is Germans, mon. Now, give me some change, will ya' mon?"

And, the guy was right in what he told you. The 500 Germans who set up a colony in Jamaica have mostly disappeared—as Germans, and as white people.

They've been taken over by alien (to them) genes and they've been zombified or made to be something that they weren't. Just about all that remains of the white Germans are some old photos and furniture and of course the German names that the blacks now have. Today, most of the former Germans have blended and are now blacks. Their assimilation, with a few exceptions, into the black masses of Jamaica is just about complete.

Apparently, the German whites resisted intermarriage for years, but now in Jamaica as in much of the rest of the world, the pressures to intermarry are intense and any desire to remain separate is considered "racist." In a few more years, there should be no more even partially white Germans left in Jamaica.

This raises the question as to whether one is truly what one was if one is no longer like what one was. In other words, is a German a German if all that remains is the family name? Is a white a white, if he or she is black? At first glance the questions may seem absurd, but they have metaphysical ramifications. When are we ourselves? When are we not ourselves? Are we ourselves if we are not really ourselves? What makes US, us? It goes on and on, but the simple answer is probably the most common sense one. These Jamaicans are not white nor are they German. The genes that made them German in the past were long ago replaced in the gene pool, never to return. Those Germans who moved to Jamaica were taken over and transformed by alien genes. Unlike the movies, however, the alien genes didn't just change them inside, but outside as well. The white ancestral chain was broken.

The process in Jamaica is very similar to what happened to many American Indians in the U.S. who intermarried with whites and thus slept their way to their own genocide.

The alien genes have found a much better way to take over and replicate themselves than by being attached to the back of someone's neck as we often seen in some science fiction movies. They do it by causing people to mate in such ways that these alien genes are inserted into a population of people where they replicate and expand with each new birth.

The truth of this invasion is that those individuals who are first taken over, remain as they are because genetically they remain the same. It is their minds that are taken over with notions that mating outside the race is okay. As individuals, they live out their lives as they were born. It's their family lines that will be changed or zombified and transformed into something that is different as they have children.

UNITY

Hardly a day goes by that we don't read about some Latino or Hispanic conference someplace in the country where the speakers call for Latino or Hispanic unity.

Who do you think Latinos are unifying against? Can't guess? Look in the mirror. They're unifying against European-Americans. Latinos are trying to transform the European-American based United States into a new Latin America. To this end, they're trying to replace European-Americans in leadership positions in all areas of life, with Latinos.

Have you heard about any white leaders meeting with white groups or white students to tell them that they must unify for their common interest and that they must be proud of their heritage and learn about and understand their heritage?

I won't hold my breath while you ponder.

Time's up. You know you haven't heard of any prominent whites doing this. Instead, you've probably seen white leaders running from their heritage and trying in thousands of little ways to deny that they even have a heritage that could be called "white." So, while white elites are saying that white ethnicity/race doesn't matter and should be ignored, Latinos are agreeing that whites should ignore white ethnicity/race and not unify as whites, but that Latinos should feel pride in their race/ethnicity and should unify as Latinos. The same white elites who downplay the importance of a white identity then, as President Clinton once did, praise Latinos for their pride and gush that "More and more, America will look like you." Clinton also gushed over the fact that whites aren't in a majority in Hawaii. Self-group hate and loathing seem to be common among such white elites.

Many whites say things such as "Why don't you drop the hyphens and stop calling us European-Americans." These folks just don't get it. While they're trying to be race neutral and trying to include all other racial/ethnic groups in any organizations that they belong to, other racial/ethnic groups understand that in order to have unity and protect their interests they must be exclusive and make distinctions between those who are members of the genetic group and those who aren't. In other words, these other racial/ethnic groups are defining themselves and are seeking to be dealt with by government and business as members of a particular ethnic/racial group, not as "just Americans," while some dopey whites are seemingly trying to destroy their chances in life by denying themselves the unity that is found in the first and most important unifying aspect of their existence—their birth into their distinct genetic group.

The effect of this is that Latinos are trying to push European-Americans out of positions of power and influence by attacking racially non-conscious European-Americans with a unified Latino front. The European-Americans, not seeing themselves as members of a distinct people, fail to see the concerted attack on "their" people and instead often think all this is just a matter of other individuals simply moving up the ladder of success, and pushing out other "individuals" who aren't as competent. In other words, many of these non-conscious European-Americans, fail to see the racial/ethnic nature of the attack and if they are downsized out of work they just figure that they're defective as individuals. At the same time, many elite liberal European-Americans are actually trying to help Latinos push European-Americans out. Such elites remind one of prisoners of war who help the enemy dig the graves of their fellow prisoners of war.

Not seeing oneself as a European-American or white, is to have a losing mental attitude that prevents one from seeking unity with those like oneself, because with this mental attitude—this aberration—one can't even recognize like from unlike. Unity requires that one be able to make such a distinction. Too many whites are alienated from who and what they truly are, and they're blind to the fact that they're alienated. One of the signs of this alienation is indicated by the aforementioned messages from whites who want to be "just Americans." In a world where people define themselves by race/ethnicity, "just American," is a loser.

Take a look at the anti-immigration forces in this country. So fearful are they that they'll be called "racists" that they waste time and energy in trying to deny that most of their members are European-Americans. Look also at some other groups with local agendas. Recently, there have been Confederate Flag rallies in some southern states. Again, so afraid of being called racists, are some of the whites behind these rallies, that they badmouth various other whites who want to speak at the rallies lest the organizers be smeared with the hate terms that these other whites have been painted with by haters of all white people. In effect this allows the haters of white people to define white people, and to keep them from finding unity.

There was a controversy a couple of years ago when a politician suddenly became the Hitler of the month after publishing a book about World War II that questioned some long held assumptions.

No doubt, some neutral, race whipped whites then distanced themselves from the politician because of the smears. The timidity and cowardice of white people—to being white people—seems to border on mass neurosis.

Few whites dare to organize and meet together as white people without putting a few non-whites in the front row to prove that the whites aren't racists. Oftentimes, the result of such blended organizations is that they're ineffective in protecting the rights of whites because, on the one hand, whites are uncomfortable in talking candidly in front of non-whites and thus mute what they want to say and on the other hand the organization lacks a natural unity by including people who are not European-Americans.

The heart-felt opinions of European-Americans are also diluted by the very presence of non-European-Americans.

HOMELESS JACK TALKS RACISM AND RELIGION

"Some numbnut asked me if I'm a racist," said Homeless Jack. "Most of the time when someone asks such a stupid question that's none of their business, I just tell them to stuff it and I don't play their game, 'cause they usually have an agenda and these days many of them are hateful and bigoted genocidists who are just trying to kill off white people in all ways possible. Their intolerant name calling and brow beating is just part of their agenda. It ain't gonna work, man. It ain't gonna work. Some of us know the truth and we're keeping the light alive. But this time I figured I'd go along, so I asked the guy to define the term racist. He said 'it means you hate people of other races.' I told him that I don't hate people of other races or other religions or other anything. The question got me thinking, though, about race and religion, 'cause the two are intertwined. Now, one's religious views are one's own business and nobody else's business, but I figure true religion is all encompassing and others often try to butt into it with questions, like this guy asked me, that on the surface may not seem to be religious questions, but which really are.

"So I told him that true science tells us that the different races are genetically different from each other in many ways and that no one with eyes to see can deny the differences and that true religion is scientific. He then said if I meant skin color that this was just a minor difference. I told him that's the way it works in nature. Seemingly minor things at this end of the microscope, so to speak, are magnified into very major things at the other end. Minor differences in the genes equal major differences as the genes are expressed. After all, we're all composed of the same basic chemicals and we all arose from the same general principles and processes. So, in one sense we're all alike, but if we want to help evolution and our purpose along, then we need to recognize the differences and we need to emphasize the differences in such a way that we can all fulfill our destinies as God or nature has intended.

"Look, everything is spinning and turning and that causes change. Only things that have no spinning or turning don't change. The cosmos is a self ordering and self organizing system and it does it all by spinning. Give DNA a little spin this way and you have this type of creature, spin it just a bit this other way and you've got something else all made from the same stuff. It's all the same, but it's all different. I figure that at the center is the One that started the spinning. Think of that One as an explosion or the natural workings of the cosmos or whatever, it doesn't matter. You might even think of that One as the axle of existence and the mouth of the tornado and the cosmic hurricane. He or she or it is the furnace of creation and destruction. But you know what? I bet if we could ever penetrate to the center we wouldn't find anything different, just more of the same like when you penetrate to the center of an onion.

Am I a racist? Nope. The concept is wrong. I don't hate anyone or anything. Even the other term "racialist," which is sometimes defined as a person who recognizes that races are different but who doesn't hate others of other races, doesn't really describe me completely. It's too small a term and is too limited to really be some sort of all encompassing religious definition, and what I believe can't be defined except in religious terms. So, race and genes are part of the larger reality, but they ain't all of it and anyone who bases his religion solely on them has too small a vision of reality. You see pictures of those spinning galaxies far away in space? The same basic thing is in every cell of our body but much smaller.

"Everything changes. Inert chemicals change and they evolve sometimes into life. What are we? We're all animated dirt, that's what. And humans are also thinking dirt. Life evolves sometimes to higher life or sometimes it devolves to lower life or sometimes it changes and the changes make it extinct eventually or sometimes it changes and you don't see much difference. We start as dirt and we end up as dirt and we're dirt in between. But, when we're in between we're dirt that thinks and reproduces. One thing is certain, and don't forget this, all of existence is spinning in space and time and this creates a spiral spinning from the smallest things to the largest. It's in the living and in the unliving and this ensures that nothing stays the same for long. It makes everything change. It builds and it destroys through all eternity using the same material over and over again.

"Nope. I'm not a racist. Maybe what I am is a spiralist or a differentialist or an essentialist. I don't know what a good term would be, but this is my religion."

"Are you getting this stuff from that book you mentioned to me before?" I asked.

"Yup."

"You said you wanted me to type it or do something with it, so where is it? When can I see it?"

"When Arman says the time is right."

"Who's Arman?"

"Never mind. That just slipped out. Forget I said it. It's not yet time. I'll let you know when it's time."

"See, if you want to talk about true religion you have to talk about life and if you talk about life you have to talk about man and if you talk about man you have to talk about races and genes and all the rest. They're all part of religion. If your religion ignores them, then it ain't true religion at all. Let me skip ahead and give you a taste of this in a slightly different way. Stay with me now. See, most white people are a little like possums. They just don't get it, and they do things that will lead to their extinction. It's not that they're stupid, exactly, but their programming is wrong.

"I figure that our brains have something like defaults like in computers that were built in at the time we were created or as we evolved, or whatever, and that even though the default settings have been modified some over the years, they still remain largely locked in the past when they were first created. If things progressed without man's rapid fire inventions, the defaults would have time to adjust, but because our technology moves so fast, these default settings don't always adjust in time to help us. This means that we must use our intellects to choose different custom settings and override some of the defaults. In other words we can't wait for blind evolution to change us. We have to take control and make it happen or we're gonna be extinct.

"See, it's like possums. One of their defaults is to play dead when they're frightened. God or nature gave them this default way back when most of the things that would kill possums were other animals whose own default settings were that they wouldn't eat something that they didn't kill themselves, because if something just up and died there was probably something wrong with the critter that might harm the eaters if they ate the thing. Now, that default setting worked pretty well for possums for millions of years. But now that we have automobiles and many possums live in urban areas, the automobiles just run over the playing dead possums and make them really dead. If possums were as intelligent as some humans and had higher consciousness as do some humans, then they would try to find a way to change the default setting so that they wouldn't play dead when cars came near them, but, instead, would run out of the way. However, they can't do this. That's because, as far as we know, they don't have the intelligence or the consciousness to even think along these lines. They can't override and change their default settings. Because to do this requires the ability to think as we can think. Thus, possums are left with the blind workings of nature to somehow change their default settings before so many of them are squished by cars that the critical number of possums falls below a level where they can survive as a species. Now, of course, there are other factors involved here such as nature increasing the defaults on possum birth rates to compensate for so many being killed, and other things as well, but I'm tryin' to illustrate a point here.

See white folks had our default settings set back when we lived in lands far removed from other types of humans. As a result of these settings and where we lived, we invented religions and made up laws and social structures that contemplated all people being just like us and having the same defaults as us. It's like when we zigged, most other white people also zigged and when we zagged, they zagged. Then, we invented mass transportation. Suddenly, our lands, which we had made more prosperous and desirable than the lands inhabited by the other 90% of humanity, were open to the rest of humanity that wanted the life styles and prosperity and low crime and all the rest that we had created for ourselves in our lands. What they and even most white people didn't and still don't understand is that these things were a product of our genes. We built the type of nests that our genes told us to build just as nature tells each type of bird to build a particular type of nest. It's the default settings in the genes, man. Instead of understanding that, and trying to overcome their own default settings in their genes that made their lands places to flee from, non-white people simply came to our lands, thinking what we had was a result of some accident of fate or because we had a better government or something like that. They never realized that the way we govern ourselves and our laws and how we relate to each other and the world around us is also from our genes. Anyway, our default settings weren't set right for us to survive in the midst of millions of people unlike us and this has led to a situation where we face our own extinction as we're swamped with their genes and our own low birthrates.

"I believe that white people can change our default settings and that we need to change them away from some of our defaults while leaving others intact and that's how we're going to survive.

"How do we change our defaults, you may ask? The first thing we must do is get our heads screwed on right and think correctly about ourselves, the world around us, and the cosmos. Then we need to get the right belief system and internalize it so that it will release hormones and other chemicals into our blood stream that will cause changes to us.

"How do we know the right things to do?" I asked.

"It's in that book I been tellin' you about, that I want you to organize and type."

"I'm ready Jack. Just tell me when."

"Soon. Very soon."

PART II

HOMELESS JACK'S RELIGION

HOMELESS JACK ON THE GUIDE

Don't go gettin' all twitchy over this religious stuff. Religion ain't just for neurotic pious types with prune faces who look like their shoes are too tight and who ain't been laid in years. Religion is the way you live and the way you look at existence along with some rules from the Big Guy to keep you on the straight and narrow. I ain't a big fan of religions and I figure most of 'em are man made and are designed to keep people within certain bounds for the benefit of other men. Many of them seem to be about denying life and welcoming death. Even if you ain't religious, I guess you're still religious in the way you approach life no matter how you approach it.

The way I figure it, from readin' The Guide is that God ain't a prig, and He gave us our senses to use. It's also clear, 'cause it's repeated a lot, that He doesn't want us to try to overcome the flesh that he gave us.

Before I go on, I've got to tell you what all existence looks like. I know, 'cause I've seen it. It's like trillions of vast rivers of sub-atomic particles, waves, rays, energies, beams, vibrations, forces and things we don't have names for all flowing in vast circles and spirals intersecting each other all over the place in massive and minuscule trajectories and orbits. There is no emptiness. It is all full of this massive spiraling flow that reminds me of some sort of moving tapestry with trillions of different colored threads all moving in different directions in the tapestry, but eventually all circling and turning into spirals, while the tapestry itself moves like a river that also circles and looks like a gigantic spiral or a gigantic spiral galaxy or a gigantic swastika. I believe that the spiral flow was set in motion by God who is, in a sense, a little like a man who dredges the earth and builds his own river that flows in a certain direction, and who then builds a boat and jumps in it and who is then in the flow that he, himself, created. Don't get me wrong, this don't mean that God ain't got power, but I think He also has to go with the flow that He created.

I figure that God mostly keeps us going in the right direction by the way He made and programmed us. So, He made some things pleasurable so we'd do 'em and he made some things not pleasurable so we'd avoid 'em. For example, He made sex pleasurable so we'd do it often and have lots of babies. Of course, by engineering us so that sex was pleasurable because of friction, He had to have known that there was more than one way to get that friction and that some of these ways do not produce babies and that people would also eventually begin mating willy nilly with people unlike themselves and that all of this pleasure gone awry would screw up His plan, which I figure is to have us all struggle to be the top dogs by us all having as many children as possible so that population pressures coupled with feelings of group loyalty would cause us all to compete with each other to get to the top and that this would lead to a more evolved being as the genes of one type dominated other types.

I figure that if God is as powerful and all knowing as He's supposed to be that he knew about the seeming unanticipated consequence of how sexual pleasure works, and that it really was an anticipated but unavoidable consequence of the engineering that God had to do to make us. Anyway, maybe God's way of correcting things is to give us The Guide as an instruction manual. Maybe it's like if you design an airplane that bullets will bounce off, it'll probably be too heavy to fly, so you have to make compromises and make the thing light enough so it'll fly, which means you can't make it bullet proof. Then, because an airplane can be flown both where bullets are flying and where they're not flying (sort of like our free will), the pilots need an instruction manual that tells them how to make the right choices. Perhaps something along these lines would work: "Ye Shall avoid all bullets, and not fly where they are, or We will destroy you." Maybe The Guide is like that instruction manual and is supposed to help us avoid the problems that can result if we use our sexual equipment in the wrong way or if we do other things in life the wrong way.

I also figure, and this goes along with I said above, that God ain't no prissy gardener making a manicured little garden, but that he casts seeds far and wide so things will grow in great profusion all a jumble and I think God loves the sheer seeming chaotic growth and the struggle of all that exists. I figure that God is something of a randy type and that his act of creation is somethin' like reproducing is for other critters and that He gets pleasure out of it and wanted to share that pleasure with everything He created and that's why He has all living things do the same thing in their own ways.

You'll go nuts if you try to figure all this stuff out, because the logic is the logic of God. Now, if you don't like that word God, then just substitute nature. The Big Wheel may not mind too much, because He says that His laws are spun in nature. So, I guess if it were possible to discover and fully understand all His laws in nature, and if you obeyed these natural laws, then you'd be in tune with God and you might not need any words to tell you what He says is right. Maybe not, though, 'cause He's blessed us with big brains so we can think different things and thus have some modicum of free will. That's also our curse, 'cause there are always two sides of every coin. The other side of our big brain coin is the curse that we can make wrong choices. The kind of critters we are with the kind of brains we have requires that we have words and symbols to know the real laws of nature and not be distracted with false ones and by the lies of evil-doers. Just 'cause we can do somethin,' don't make that an acceptable law of nature. See, one example of this is the fact that we can mate with critters who ain't exactly like us and produce children, but that don't mean that's okay with God, 'cause it ain't.

There are hidden psychological things about humans that require their religions to be a certain way and to have certain things. If they don't have these things, they ain't gonna work and they're gonna die off and be dead religions or other religions are goin' to run right over 'em. Sometimes, people have taken religious things and tried to strip them of the religious stuff and sell them as philosophical or social or political things. Big mistake. The longest lasting philosophical products of the minds of men, that actually move men in large numbers, are religions. Take understanding from this and open your minds. Overcome that skeptical part of your minds and don't intellectualize this stuff too much. If you want to learn, you have to drop your mental defenses and just be sponges. Let it all seep in and maybe you'll feel that wind from out of the far places and maybe you'll find true happiness in this life after you are in tune with the ultimate and the flow of existence as it spirals around in endless circles within circles with meanings within meanings and with things that look like this, but which are really that.

Now, here's the stuff that's probably gonna piss a lot of people off: This ain't a religion for everybody and it's different from all other religions. You gotta have the right stuff inside you for this to be your religion just like a radio has to have the right stuff to pick up radio waves. If you ain't got the right tubes or transistors, you don't get the radio waves. That's just the way it is. God is the God of all that exists, but He made things different and with different purposes that We don't understand. He's the God of the fish in the sea and the birds in the sky as much as He's the God of us, but He didn't give us gills or wings. Instead, he gave Essence to some of us humans and He didn't give it to any other type of humans. He gave them other gifts. If you don't have the right stuff, take it up with God.

Anyway, here's the stuff that I found in a dumpster. As I said before, I figure this book was put in my path by that guy I bought some food for. It's typed up all pretty so it's easy to read and that's a hell of a lot better than the crappy pages I found which were all messed up. A lot of stuff is repeated in here, especially 'bout having lots of kids. I didn't know whether I should try to edit the material or just leave it as I found it. I finally just left it as I found it, except that a lot of the pages were loose, so I just kinda closed my eyes and put them back in. I left it up to the Big Guy to get the order right. The more I read this thing, the more I find. It's almost though God is ahead of us in the forest and is secretly giving us clues about which path to follow. Over here there are some bread crumbs. Over there is a little mark on a tree. Then there's a couple of stones on top of each other. It's up to us to look for His clues and to stay on the path. We don't ever really see Him, just His clues. I figure that sometimes He's something of a trickster with a sense of humor.

I already told you that this is my religion, but if you ask me about it sometime, I might just tell you that what I believe ain't none of anyone's business and that it's between God and me or, if the mood hits me, I might tell you this ain't my religion. It's my choice what I say, 'cause I can choose.

THE GUIDE

GOD IS GREAT!

God willing, these words given by God will find their way into the hands, the minds and the hearts of all who have the Essence and who know that He alone is God and that He alone shall determine the fate of peoples as He alone wishes.

THE SYMBOL

Believe what you read herein and do what you are told to do and do not do what is forbidden.

This book is a guide for your existence. Seek answers herein often and study these words, for there are meanings within meanings for those with the Essence to understand.

Say: It was God who came with light and sound to that which was dark and silent.

Say: It was God who made the point that was the start of the spinning and it is God who causes the spinning and the spiral of existence.

Say: It was God who started all. It was God who made all that is seen and all that is unseen. It was God who gave you life and made you more than the chemicals that make up your bodies. It was God who caused intelligence, awareness and consciousness to grow from dust and move ever higher from one form to another up the spiral.

It was God who has sent you symbols of the spinning so that in them you may think of Him and be guided in your understanding of what He wants of you.

It was God who commanded that in the trailing armed spinning form is He to be seen in His most glorious aspect.

It was God who commanded that believers have this symbol with them every moment that their form is in existence both living and dead.

Holy are those who cause this symbol to be upon their skin so that it cannot be removed and so that it serves as a sign to believers and non-believers alike that the bearer obeys Us and will be protected by Us from evil.

When you gather together to worship God, erect this symbol upon your alter and look upon this symbol with great reverence and set before it a fire and growing things.

Fight against those who hate God and who hate His symbols and do not let them keep you from openly displaying your love for God by displaying His symbols. Those who seek to harm God or His believers are evil, no matter what other good they claim to do. They are to be kept from ever carrying out their harmful thoughts.

We command you to obey and honor Us and to display Our symbols for the world to see and to not let any men or governments of men deny you what We have ordained. Display Our spirals in all their forms wherever you may dwell or travel and know that We see Our symbols and We will protect you for bearing Our symbols as signs of your faith and obedience. Allow none to defile or insult Our symbols. Primary among the representations of Our symbols is the spiraling four armed form, for it represents Us in Our most active form and it must be displayed at the most sacred times and days and it must especially be displayed wherever there are haters of Us and evil-doers for it is protection against their evil. Display it proudly but without false and arrogant pride in your heart so that all may know that We are God and We alone will determine what is proper and what is not proper for Our believers.

Carry this symbol before you when you face the evil-doers and it shall be a beacon and a light to Our Shining Ones who shall aid you against those who hate you and Us and who seek to destroy you.

We have made you a peaceful and a just people and We command you to be thus and to spend your lives in worship of Us in all the things that you do and no matter where you live or travel, but We warn you that there are those who are evil and they will attempt to destroy you. Do not show a peaceful face to evil-doers, but be as ravening wolves. Make war to protect the faith and the faithful and if any try to harm the faith or the faithful by word or deed or by devious means or through clever plots, then they are to be made war upon by all means necessary until they can never again harm you. Just as We have many faces, so too must you have many faces. We make and destroy and remake trillions of stars to fulfill Our plan and We are the spinning and We are the spun. We are the center and We are the arms trailing. Our plan will unfold as We alone have decreed. So too do you play a part in Our plan. As We are, you must be. We have made you our representatives on the worlds to do there as We wish and command. Our ways are your true natural ways for We have made and selected you to be thus alone among all others. There are none but you who We have selected and you are alone and separate even in the midst of others as We are alone and separate.

THE STRUGGLE

We have created you to struggle all the days of your life and to walk your own steps. We have given you the legs and the feet, but you must take the steps. We have given you a brain, but you must think the thoughts. We have given you choices, but you must choose. We wait and We watch how you choose. Choose wisely and you shall be blessed, for We are compassionate and just. Choose unwisely and you shall be punished, for We weigh all that you do.

Love the struggle and, God willing, you shall know happiness. Hate the struggle and you shall be unhappy all the says of your life.

There is no final destination for you in flesh, only eternal change. We have set your genes within you to compete with all other genes for dominance. The conflict that so results is a natural part of Our order and is eternal. You shall be changed as the gene wars continue and it is up to you to be changed either toward the light or away from it. Although you are directed by your genes in many ways, We have given you the knowledge of this fact so that you may set your genes to take the right path toward Us. For while your genes move blindly, We have given you eyes to see the path and the ability to direct the course of your genes. When you consciously control the destiny of your genes, you shall control the destiny of yourself and Our Essence shall prevail.

THE GUIDE

All praise to God who hath made us as we are and who allows us to become more if we follow His guide.

Follow not the false religions for they shall lead you astray and they will lead you to your doom. God despises the false religions and non-believers who have Essence but who waste their Essence in false beliefs and in false living.

God has set forth the inner light, and He has set the light in a people who alone are His people and who alone will He guide ever higher so long as they believe.

God is the God of all existence, but all of existence is not the same in the eyes of God, for God has made all things different but has formed all from the same material. Is your fingernail the same as your hair? Is your spleen the same as your brain? Is your foot the same as your ear? All are a part of you, but all are different. God willing, you shall understand this about all that God has made.

Say: There is but one God and He is within and He is without. He alone makes holy and blessed what He wills. He has set the trajectory that existence now follows and has started the flow.

Say: All things in existence now or which ever were in existence or which ever will be in existence have a purpose and God alone knows the purpose of all things and reveals only what He wishes to reveal.

THE FLESH

You are your flesh and your flesh is you. They are inseparable. Your spirit arises from your flesh and is a product of your flesh. With different flesh your spirit is different. Seek to preserve and improve your flesh. We alone determine when species arise and when they die. We alone set forth all things to struggle. We alone have started the sacred spinning. We alone have ordained what is built and what is destroyed by the sacred spinning.

Those that do not correctly struggle cease to exist for We give no gifts of eternity to those not willing to ensure their survival.

Many are the those who misuse what We have given you and they disobey Our laws thinking that their false ideas of Us are correct and that their false ideas of Us accepts them no matter what evil they do. They are wrong and We shall punish them for their arrogance. They are as fingernails or hair to Us and We cut them off and throw them out with no loss to Us. What We throw out is destroyed in this form and is returned to a lower form lacking life and it becomes material and fuel for what new things We create. All that exists is a part of Us and arose from Us as We so willed, but different things have different purposes. We have ordained an Order that is known only to Us.

We have given you your senses so that you can use them as We have willed them to be used. Do not deny your senses or you deny Us, and this is evil for We will not be denied.

We have caused inert matter to evolve to flesh so that flesh would give rise to brains so that brains would give rise to minds so that minds would be conscious and would wonder about Us and seek Us. Say to the believers: "Do you seek the flesh of God? You shall not find it, for God is mind without flesh."

Think not that all of reality is an illusion. It is not. Your senses tell the truth as We want you to see the truth. We have given you senses to see, hear, smell, taste and feel so that you can know this thing from that thing and this living creature from that living creature. Do you not know that We can give other senses, if We so will? You see, hear, smell, taste and feel, but you do not hear, smell, taste or feel all, for only We can sense all the parts of existence and how they are connected.

Evil are those who deny their senses and who say "We must must ignore the differences between different living things."

Your flesh has become contaminated and impure and this dooms you to short lives and much disease and it keeps you from truly knowing what We want you to know and keeps you from hearing Us as we whisper to your Essence. We are compassionate and We have given you these words so that you may remove the contamination and impurities and become as We wish you to be. Few are they who are blessed to hear Us through their Essence, and We have selected only one who has the hidden sense within to hear Us clearly and to understand and write these words so others can use their sense of sight to see these words with their own eyes and in seeing, take these words into their brains. Understand these words and what is written invisibly in between these words and follow the righteous path to understanding.

WILL O' WISP

We are here and there at the same time. None but Us can be thus. Our consciousness is in a speck of dust that you walk upon and it is in the clouds in far away space, and it is whole and complete in each. Both are the same to Us. Where the spinning spiral form exists, We exist. See Our face in the in the whirlwind. Evil are they who ignore the spinning.

We are the One who has made life. It was We who made man. And, what are you, you who think that you are your own masters? You are dirt that We have spun together so that you possess Our gift of life. We have put the life-force within. You are chemicals and electrical processes and vibrations and waves and forces and particles that are held together by the spinning. Should We stop the spinning, all would cease to be.

We are the One who cannot be seen directly, but We are here and there and everywhere just beyond what you can see. You look upon Us, but you do not see Us.

We have been here before time began and We shall be here when time ends and We shall begin it all over again. We cannot be destroyed. We are the builder and the destroyer of all. We are God. From out of the mouth of Our spiral does all come and does all return.

CHANGE

You have worshiped false Gods, made by man, in the image of man, to do the bidding of man. This is now to come to an end. There is no God but Us and there is no version of God but what We tell you. All other gods are false. All other versions are lies. There can be no compromise with non-believers about Our nature. We are not a committee. We are not your servant. We are not your fantasy. We do not negotiate. We do not compromise. We do not seek to be as you wish. We are God. We have put a special spark of Us in your people alone. No other people possess this spark nor will they ever possess it. You, alone, have Our special attention. Think not that We can't remove that spark or that We won't remove that spark if you do not give up evil ways. We are compassionate and we are just, but We will be obeyed.

You who believe, be guided and take up the cause. Help each other build temples and circles and places of worship where you may gather to worship Us and where you gain strength from the collective power of Us arising from Our special spark in you that passes through your flesh and combines with the spark that has passed through the flesh of all believers and combines and returns to make them more powerful. Destroy the false gods and their evil images for they are an affront to Us. Make small temples to Us where you live so that you are never far from a temple, and pray before the small temple when you cannot pray in larger temples. Kneel before Us and focus your thoughts on Us and pray that We will not remove the spark. Sanctify your temples with Our symbols. Join together in organizations within organizations and build large temples and centers and have them be places full of believers and life and light at all times, and make them not like the false buildings used by non-believers that are devoid of life.

THE NAME OF GOD

We are all names and We are no names. When We willed Our existence as We now are, We occupied all that exists.

We have set a part of Our Essence in you and it is the spark of Us and the part of you that is Us that makes you special in all of creation.

We have given you the right blood through your lines and we give you the right belief through these words. You must protect and multiply both by right actions for We have given you this responsibility.

No other people is as beloved to Us as you. And, no other people angers Us more than those who have Our special gift who disrespect Us.

You have fallen from Our grace by allowing your blood and your world to become infected with other blood and other beliefs. This is evil, but We are a compassionate God and We will let you correct your wrongs and make things right. You must purify to realize your potential in Us. We are compassionate and hold back our destroying arm for love of you, but We will destroy all if you do not make the right choices of your own free will.

And, the people ask: 'How far have we strayed from the righteous path?" Answer them in Our name: 'Know that We have set your life span at 1200 years and your impurity keeps you from living your full life span and truly knowing Us. Your short lives are but one mark of how far you have strayed. When you are purer, you shall know Us better and you shall know Our grace and you shall live according to Our clock within you. You are now born as children and you die as children with barely a tenth of the life span that We have ordained. You must purify to come close to Us.'

GOOD AND EVIL

The people ask: "What is good and what is evil?"
Answer them: What God says is good is good.
What God says is evil is evil.

Good and evil are not to be determined by any but God.

Many people, because of arrogance and false beliefs say this is good or this is evil when the opposite is true.

We have given you this guide so that you may know what is good and what is evil and so that you alone of all peoples may walk the road that We demand you walk.

Abandon false ideas of man and follow what We demand or you shall perish and be as dust on the road that others shall walk.

THE REVELATIONS

We reveal what We wish to reveal in ways that We wish. We speak through the natural things for those who can truly know Us. Those who see Us as We truly are become as madmen. These are the ones whose Essence touches Our Essence from time to time and who are surprised to suddenly know what others do not know. Should their Essence touch our Essence too much, they become as a burned bush. We speak Our subtle ways through music and images and words and breezes and the storms and the living things lest We burn believers. Who has the truth of Us? Those whose Essence is purer. No humans but your people have Essence and none have Essence that is pure. Some are more pure than others and some are more impure than others. When your ancestors came to forks in the road they chose unwisely and they doomed you to impurity and short lives. We have put signs both seen and unseen upon your flesh and in your bodies so that the faithful may be guided in this. We have set forth ideals in the flesh to be copied and followed. You must purify your Essence to know Us. You are to multiply those with the purer Essence in all ways possible. Say to the people this simple thing that they may remember: 'You must purify, protect, propagate, persevere, perfect, preserve, prevail.' The Essence We first gave to a single man and a single woman must be multiplied by multitudes of children. We have given you the means and the desire within your bodies to pass on the Essence. With each child of believers does the Essence spread. Evil are they who do not spread the Essence by having as many children as their bodies will allow. Do not study your potential mates overlong but satisfy yourself that your mate is of the people. This is enough. We shall correct as We shall correct when there is a vast multitude of your people stretching from horizon to horizon with none but your people in sight. When your people are so numerous and vigorous that they are as a roiling mass of maggots devouring the rotting flesh of those who must pass from this existence you shall be closer to Us. Do not be offended, for We love life that is numerous and vigorous and full of growth and expansion and that will not be denied and which does not beg for existence but demands it as a right that We have given to those who will take it.

You shall find immortality in the flesh according to the number of children you bring forth who are as pure or purer than you. Your Essence stores up your good and bad deeds and these things are passed on to your children in the Essence that you pass on. You have your Essence through your birth. There is no other way. We maintain the scales and We weigh the good you do and the bad you do and we reward and punish fairly as the scales tip. Each child you produce weighs ten times more on the scale of good than any other good that you do. Much bad that you do can be erased by having great numbers of children and it is the wise believer who balances the scales with many children.

THE SEED

Say to the believers in Our name: 'You are the carriers of Our eggs and Our seed. It is your duty and responsibility to protect and multiply them.'

God willing, you shall have so many children that each family shall become a tribe and a nation. God willing, all believers shall be one and the one that is shall be a vast multitude so that believers shall dominate all the worlds for the glory of God.

Say to the believers: 'A person who could have had children but who dies childless has dishonored Us. Such a person might as well have not lived at all.

Say to the believers: 'A person who causes Our sacred seeds or eggs to become polluted is an abomination in the eyes of God.'

Do you not know that Our truths are in your bodies? We have written them there in the spiral within. We have made you to be able to do Our will and fulfill your duty. A fool does not believe our natural law, but a believer does.

Say to the fool: 'You doubt the natural law of God? Can you not see how this law is written in the cosmos and in your flesh? If you aim a blow at a man's head, arm, legs, trunk, he'll only flinch a little. Aim a blow at his groin and he'll double over instantaneously to avoid harm to his seed. But you fools say that this is only natural because it hurts more if he's hit in his organs of reproduction than in other places. This is true and it is true precisely because God has made it more painful to be hit there so that you will protect His seeds and His eggs. This is how God writes his laws in your flesh. Take understanding from this in all things.'

Say to the non-believer who has the right blood: 'You do not understand God's laws because you do not try to understand. You have hardened your heart and your mind. Take your lesson from these words.'

Say to the people: 'God is economical in what He designs. He does not do things for no reason. Nor does he over engineer what He creates. Your brain remains as a child's brain all the days of your short life because you do not live to your full life span. God has given you a natural life span of 1200 years, not your present 80 years. Your Essence is impure and you live a short life and you do not reach your full potential. Few can understand a scintilla of God's truths until they are 400 years old. Who now lives to this age? You are as infants all the days of your life. You are born not knowing and you grow old and die not knowing and when you die, you are as ignorant as the moment you were born.'

Say to the people: 'Your purpose in having the ability to breed is to breed. You must pass on as many of your genes as possible so that your genes will dominate all other genes. Each person is commanded to do this. Thus is there a competition established that will lead to the best being dominant. Man is an animal who can override some of his instincts in the short run and in so doing, man can frustrate the purpose for his existence if he overrides what must not be overridden and if he fails to override what must be overridden. You must rid yourselves of false teachings and evil ways and you must follow this Guide, for it will show you the path and will keep you from overriding proper instincts and angering Us and not overriding what must be overriden in the times in which you live. When you are in doubt, this Guide shall show you the way.'

All things are interconnected and there are effects that happen over there that also happen over here, but what happens over there changes other things and it is like balls hitting other balls and causing all sorts of effects. Only God can foresee all that happens there from the slightest movement here, and only God can ensure that everything that happens works for His plan.

THE WOLF AND THE SHEEP

A wolf is a wolf even though he thinks he is a sheep. If he thinks he is a sheep and tries to be a sheep, he will be a very bad sheep. He will be unhappy and never be satisfied because he is trying to go against his nature that God has written in him. He can only be happy by being what he truly is. Take understanding from this, you who deny these truths and who mock God and His believers.

CHILDREN

We love life and We love the children of the people We have selected. It is pleasing to Us to look upon a land that is teeming with Our children and it is not pleasing to Us to look upon a barren land or barren people or lands teeming with others who, by their presence, come between you and Us. Say to those who are intentionally barren: 'Get away from us, for you are evil and you are useless. You are full of death and decay. Your presence is an affront to God. We choose to surround ourselves with those who are full of life and growth. Blow away as the dead leaves of autumn, you foolish childless ones. You are evil in the eyes of God for you were given precious life so you could carry and spread God's Essence through His seeds and His eggs, but you have wasted your lives and have not spread God's Essence, and in this have you disobeyed God's first law. You shall have no eternal life in any form. You are nothing more than the dust under foot. You are dead though you still breathe. God's seed and eggs lie rotting within you. If God has made you so that you cannot physically bear children, then you shall still be beloved of God and a part of His plan, for He has determined who shall and who shall not bear His eggs and His seeds to birth.

Say to those who have many children with the Essence: 'You are beloved of God and even if you stray a little from the sacred path, you are holier than most and you shall live forever so long as your children and their children and their children through the ages are believers. But should your children or their children or their children through the ages fall away from belief and become one with the others, as many have in the past, then you shall die and they shall find that their lives are shorter than the lives of believers who have not become one with the others.'

The people ask: 'What is the proper age that is set by God for us to have children?"

Answer them thus in Our name: 'It is written in your Essence. It is the age when your body can have children. Serve and obey God always and follow His laws all the days of your life. God willing, you shall bear a multitude of children and your family shall become a tribe and a nation. God has placed His clock within you and His clock is law.'

WILL YOUR EVOLUTION

We have set you on the path to perfection. You must walk the path. Do not believe the science of man when it conflicts with Our truths for such science is false. We are the source of all true science and all true science is as We set forth. You can improve your Essence if you have right blood and then have right belief and right actions. Each birth can make your line purer or less pure or have it remain the same. Seek to obtain more of the right blood in your line so that your line's Essence is turned toward right belief and right actions. Gaze often upon Our symbols, for they have the power to transform you. And should you bear Our symbols around your neck or on your fingers, then have them be raised so that you may touch them and feel closer to Us. Allow only believers of skill to make such representations of Our symbols and let those who make them, pray over them so that they shall be blessed.

You must avoid all substances that will harm your Essence. If your body is harmed, your Essence is also harmed.

Your people have polluted the Essence through many means including sinful mating. This has caused you to fall from the sacred glowing path. Believers alone among all humans have the right Guide to remove the pollution.

JOIN TOGETHER

Believers are to join together to worship Us whenever this is possible. Build circles open to the sky where this can be done and have standing stones that the believers may touch. Surround yourself with Our living plants that grow naturally and do not seek to make these things orderly, but let them be wild. In the wild spontaneous growth and the struggle to exist do We find beauty and there is order in seeming disorder and if you cannot see it, it is because you are imperfect. We are circles and wheels and spirals. We create thus. Look at the wild growing things. They make a pattern with Our invisible hand that We can see and which We love. Our life force is in the circular and spiral forms and shapes. Our symbol shall protect and lead you. Let all your senses know Us.

THE ROSE

We have given you flesh and genes and all the things of substance and We have put in them all your senses so that you may do Our will. So, why are you so easily led astray by evil-doers who tell you that flesh must be denied and that your senses don't matter?

Why do you so easily believe that you have a separate spirit within you that is the real you?

We know the answer. You are imperfect. We know your imperfections but We are compassionate and kind. Your ability to be led astray is a part of the free will that We have given you. We have given you the power to think for yourselves. You can think good thoughts, and you can think bad thoughts. We have lifted you above other creatures by giving you this power. We gave you the ability to ponder and reflect and think about things beyond the basic things needed for survival. We created you so that you could either find your way up or find your way down. Because We are compassionate We have brought you these words to guide you so that you may know the difference between right and wrong and so that you can choose for yourself. These words reveal some of Our plan to those who can understand. We know your limitations and your faults. You can follow Our plan of your own free will and become more, or you can go on other paths that will lead to your destruction.

Foolish are those who teach evil things about the spirit and try to make you overcome the flesh that We have given you, while pretending that they are not evil. They try to lead you off the true path and into evil by their lies. We shall punish such ones for the evil they do.

Say to these evil ones: 'Saying that the spirit is the real you is like saying the scent of a rose is the real rose. If you want a sweeter smelling rose, you do not work directly on the scent in the air, but on the rose itself. A healthy, youthful rose will naturally have a pleasant scent for that is its nature. Purify the physical and all that arises from the physical will be purified. The song of a song bird is not the bird.'

SEPARATE

You are the Rif. Tell the believers that they are to be separated out from the non-believers and make between them and others barriers that none may cross. We want Our people pure so that they may do Our work. You are to serve only Us.

At times and in places where complete separation is not possible, according to Our law, keep your homes and your temples pure and allow no others who do not have the Essence to enter therein for this is a sacrilege and an abomination. If this happens, you must immediately purify the polluted areas with water and soap and bleach. The very air itself in such places is polluted by others and must be cleaned by passing much air through the area. Our Shining Ones can sense the presence of others and they are angered in Our name.

You carry Our sacred seeds and sacred eggs within your bodies that must be joined to bring forth more of you in great numbers so that the grains of sand on all the beaches will envy your numbers.

FYLFOT

Take this four armed symbol, this Fylfot, and display it so that the Shining Ones may see you as one who obeys Us and respects Us.

And, if evil-doers persecute you for bearing Our symbol, they prove thereby that they are enemies both of God and believers and they must not be tolerated.

Woe be to them who do this. We do not forget and We do not let wrongs go unpunished.

If the haters demand that you not wear this sacred symbol on rings or clothes or pendants or bracelets or display it in all places, do not do as they wish. Holy are they who bear this symbol on their flesh so that all may see and know them as holy and obedient to Us. Our symbol is essential to this faith We have given to you and it shall be ever so. You cannot pray or please Us, unless you display Our symbol. And, the evil-doers will come to the people and they will try to trick the people into not displaying Our sacred symbol and failing that, they will try to force the people to not display Our symbol. Do not let the evil-doers keep you from Our symbol and do not be so arrogant as to think that you may compromise in Our name over Our symbol so that you will not offend others. Believers who say they believe, but who refuse to display Our symbol out of fear or for other reasons, are not true believers.

You who display our symbols and fight against the evil-doers will be known as righteous and We will protect you all the days of your life. Gaze upon Our symbol in times of stress and weakness and it shall give you strength. Do not be caught without this symbol upon you.

When We gaze over the worlds of man and when We send our Shining Ones to destroy the evildoers, We shall look for Our symbol. Do not be where this symbol is not to be seen. Put it upon your homes and your bodies and your vehicles so that you shall be spared.

Who would deny you this symbol, would harm Our people. Holy are believers who avenge all wrongs against Us to the tenth degree. The fylfot is Our sacred symbol in motion and is the active representation of our Sacred Spiral. Where it is, We are. From its center comes all and goes all.

The people of the blood who do not yet believe, watch the early believers with a mixture or curiosity and foreboding as they watch a man dangling from a bridge. 'Will he fall? They say. 'Surely he can't survive.' But when the man falls, he is not harmed if he believes in Us. For We will cushion his fall if he is of pure heart and has followed what We have told him to follow.

And, some of these people of the blood who do not yet believe will join with the evil-doers in trying to destroy Our believers but the devious things that they plan will be seen, and it will be they who We will destroy. We shall first warn them by sending our spirals in ways that will cause them consternation and wonder. And if they do not then stop their evil, We shall send our spiral and our Shining Ones to visit every house where they live and they will know Our wrath and there shall be no place for them to hide.

Wicked people will perish by the hundreds of millions before Our wrath and they shall be as a garbage heap upon which new life shall feed. We shall send the four armed wheel in the storm and in fire to the lands where evil-doers dwell and it shall cut down the evil-doers right before your eyes. And, the people of the blood who are still non-believers shall come out of their homes and they shall prostrate themselves on the ground and beg for forgiveness for their little faith.

Wait not for Our wrath to fall upon those who hate Us and Our believers for We have anointed you as our representatives to do in your sphere where We have set you, as We do for all spheres.

If any have it in their minds and hearts to harm believers, then suffer them not, but attack and destroy them before they can act. Those who speak out against believers or who agitate against them or incite against them in order to harm them are as evil and guilty by their own acts as are those who actually harm believers.

DO GOOD

You are capable of doing good and you are capable of doing evil. We have given you the right to choose once you know the difference. You are often confused as to which is which. For this reason have We sent you this Guide: your minds respond to words and symbols. It is necessary for Us to enter into the affairs of the world to make corrections to the trajectory of those gone astray, but We do this rarely. It is for you to find the glowing path and to stay on it, with the help of this Guide.

You must avoid being deceived by the evil-doers who appear not as evil-doers. Know them by the falsehoods that they teach no matter how kindly they try to appear. Their ways will lead to your utter destruction, for if you follow them or believe as they believe, then We shall destroy you. They tell you that it is good to mix your blood with the blood of others and many believe this vile lie that leads to your destruction. To so mix your blood is to do the greatest sin against Us that is possible. Your bodies are temples to Us before all other temples. Keep them pure. Fools are they who believe that We would make physical creatures and then tell them that physical things are not important. Before you can purify yourself spiritually, you must purify yourself physically. We demand right blood as We first gave it to you when We brought you here. You have caused your blood to be impure by mating with impure beings who do not have the Essence. This has brought you low. Now you must breed away the impurities in your blood lines by proper mating and by proper belief and proper actions in all things. To wash away the impurities in your blood lines requires the birthing of children in vast numbers. We give you this Guide to help you see the way so that you may get back on the path. By following Our reveled truths, believers shall see the life spans of their lines increase. They shall also see the intelligence of their lines increase and they shall see sickness and ill health in their lines decrease. There shall come a day when ones from your lines shall be before Us in good health who are 1200 years old. And, in those days, they shall not be perfect, but they shall only be where your people were before they sinned and caused their blood to be infected, and they shall then continue to move along the path. Not all will move forward. It shall be the few who are the most righteous and the most obedient to Us who shall birth the ones to come, and the rest shall fall away and become as garbage.

Live your life in a good and just manner. Harm no living things save for food or to protect yourself and the faith. Struggle always to be pure and to prevail. Wear plain clothes that are comfortable and functional and which are made of Our soft cotton. Pray to Us at dawn as the light begins and when you feel the breeze of the new day and at twilight. Especially pray to Us during storms, for in the storms can you feel Us in your blood. Do not cover up from the winds, rain and snow except as it is necessary to protect your health. Feel the natural forces on your skin. For when you feel them, you feel Us. We are a God of movement and spinning and struggle, and We are your only God.

WOMEN

Women are the gatekeepers and protectors of Our sacred eggs. Men and women are deceived by evil-doers who come to the women and pollute and destroy their eggs. These eggs are not the possession of those who carry them any more than is the seed of men their possession. We own these things. We put them in you to carry and protect and to combine to produce more of you. We have given you what you need so that you will be the inheritors of the Earth if you but believe.

The people, deceived by evil-doers, have established false laws for the birthing of children and they have set arbitrary ages for when women and men may bring forth children. These laws are false and they keep you from bringing forth the greatest number of children. Have We not said that We have set the correct age for birthing children in your bodies? Do not waste the time given you. It is a sacred duty to bring forth as many children as your bodies can provide and you shall come to Us through your children.

These are words given by Us to help you stay on the true path to Us and so you may live your lives in accordance with Our will.

Do you not know that We have established an order of things and that it is evil for the order to be changed?

Do you think that We set all in motion just so the universe and all that is in it shall remain static and sterile and not move higher? All that exists is in motion, and all that exists changes.

We have chosen who We wish to choose and We have enlightened those who We wish to enlighten and We dim those who we wish to be dimmed.

We brought light to all that was dark. We brought life to all that was dead. We brought energy to all that had none. We brought struggle to all that wished repose. We brought wakefulness to all that slept.

We are the only God. There is no other.

Have faith in Us and praise us. Say, "God willing," often and keep Us in your thoughts and ask Us to help you, and if We do not help you, then know that you are in Our hands nevertheless and you are part of the plan that only We can understand and that Our help or lack of help is the way things must be for the larger plan to work as We have ordained.

TEMPLES

Build temples to Us and let them be places of joy and life. Let them resound with the laughter of children. Do not come to Our temples as winter, but come as spring. Come with life, not death. Come with vigor, not feebleness. Come with laughter and song. Come with joy and gusto and with a happiness and thankfulness that We have invested lifeless minerals and chemicals with Our life so that you may live to experience all that We have created through the senses We have given you.

Let a portion of Our temples be open to the forces of nature for in these forces will you feel Us. Let the temples have wild unkempt gardens with growing things of all manner. Let there be moss and ivy. Let there be trees of Oak and Ash and Birch where they may grow naturally and of other types where those grow naturally. Let the growing plants grow as they will in chaos and beauty and let them cover up things that have no life and imbue them with life. And let the believers go among the growing things and feel Our presence as We whisper out from every bush and every tree. We are in the wild things. Everything that exists is a sensor for Us.

GREATEST DUTY

Have We not said that bearing children is your greatest duty and you must bring forth as many as possible in as short a time as possible? Even if this makes you poor in earthly things it shall make you rich in Our eyes and you shall be rewarded. Evil are those who can do this, but who do not do this.

ALL ENCOMPASSING

This Guide is a holy thing and is given to you so that you may use it and be guided by the truths herein. Your faith in Us must be all encompassing. There is not a part of your existence that should be outside this belief.

LEADERS

Have We not made it plain that each of the believers has a direct and immediate relationship with Us? Right blood, right belief, right action ensure that this is so. Even so, do not hesitate to call up those from among you to help you so that you may have a human voice to listen to and a human ear to talk to in times of need, but do not make of these you call up something higher than yourself. They are helpers. When you speak to them, you are speaking to Us, but you are not speaking through them to Us, you are speaking directly to Us.

HOLIEST TIMES

Know that you can feel Us in the full force of nature for We are of nature and We started nature. Welcome the storms and the seasons and the period in the early morning just before the sun rises when night is just turning to day and when you feel the cool wind making the hairs on the back of your neck stand up and when the animals move from here to there in anticipation. Honor Us also as the sun sets. And, honor us in the fires that you keep burning in the dark of night, for We are pleased by this.

FALSE ONES

Do not be mislead, O believers, by false prophets and leaders who come to harm you. Do not be deceived. This Guide is your Guide for all times and it may never be changed. It is from Us and is written in words so that you may easily understand. It is Our way for you and it is not a human Guide but it is Our Guide and We are eternal.

Evil ones come and they say "Believers, you must not believe as you believe, because this is hateful to other humans." Say to them: 'We are believers in God, not in humans, and our beliefs are not your concern. Go from us and leave us be to worship as we wish and we shall harm you not. Go back to your false gods and your idols. Go back to worshiping humans. Go back to your evil ways and your false beliefs. You are deceived and you know it not. But, if among you there are those whose Essence is right and who hear the whisper of God, then let them take up this Guide and follow the right path.'

The spiral is sent by God. Evil are the humans who try to deny God's will. They will be punished. If you do not honor your ancestors, you shall have no descendants and you shall be struck from the face of the earth and you shall never return. Your spirit is passed on through your children and your children's children down through time. Those who are childless because their bodies cannot produce children shall also come to us and they shall be happy. Those whose bodies can produce children and who choose not to have children have chosen unwisely and there are special punishments awaiting them. Those who cause Our seed and Our eggs to produce children who are not of the blood shall be punished for their sins and they shall know oblivion.

PURIFICATION

We are a compassionate and a kind God and We warn before We destroy so those who are doing evil can correct their ways. Seek to purify the Essence of your line through your children and seek place purification through living in places inhabited only by other people of the Essence. Purest are those places where the people are both of the Essence and of the belief.

We are God and there is no other. The best and the holiest of Our people have the most children and show thereby that they understand Our law that believers are to multiply and dominate all of the universes that will ever exist. There is no other way to Us. Do not seek to make believers out of those who do not have the Essence, for this is evil and they may not worship as the believers worship nor mingle with believers. Warn non-believers with the Essence that they must come to this faith or they will perish with those with no Essence when We send our Shining Ones to destroy.

THE BUTTERFLY

God willing, you shall take understanding from these words and not be led astray into evil and extermination.

I saw a caterpillar and it was a lowly thing and I could see that if the conditions were wrong that it would always remain so until the day it dies and it would never fulfill its purpose or its destiny, and I could see that if the conditions were right; then that potential that existed within the spiral within the caterpillar would be realized and the caterpillar would transform into a butterfly; a creature so different from the caterpillar that if such did not exist in God's reality then all would claim such a thing is not possible.

And I could see other insects and crawling things gathering about the caterpillar and I could imagine that they said "Let us be as you caterpillar. Let us join your religion and live with you so that we too can be butterflies. And I could imagine the caterpillar saying :This can never be, for you lack the potential. Your spiral is different from my spiral, your essence is different from mine. The butterfly that I am to become is already within me. This I believe, but more than this, it is a physical fact that is independent of my belief. You can believe that you too possess a butterfly within you, but your belief will be as nothing, for in fact you do not have the potential.

And I could imagine I heard the other insects saying "Oh, so you think that you are better that us do you? You think that your kind is better, and that we are as nothing. How dare you think such things. Are we not all insects? Are we not therefore all alike?

And I could imagine that the caterpillar simply smiled to himself for was it not written that those who lacked the potential could never understand? The lack of potential is manifested in physical outward signs but it is also manifested in a peculiar turn of mind that blinds those without it to the truth so that they can not understand no matter how they try, what the caterpillar and believers know instinctively.

CIRCLES

Gather in circles and worship Us. Let there be stones all about and let the believers feel the winds, rain and snow upon their faces. Face the rising sun as We bring it up in the sky. Consecrate ground with a circle all about you and make of it a spiral. Find believers and join together into circles within circles to worship, for We find this fitting.

SACRED SIGNS

You carry the sacred signs inside and outside. Look for them. Seek to acquire them. Mate to improve. Preserve Our seed and Our eggs through all means possible so that long after you pass, you can still bear children. And make your homes and your temples places of light and joy and abundant life. We love the places that are full of the sounds of little children and we do not like the places that are sterile and devoid of life.

O, Believers, where you do not have a circle or a temple, fear not that this shall anger Us, for you are a walking temple and you bear upon and in your flesh our signs and if you are a true believer than you have caused our symbols to be placed upon your skin. The Shining Ones shall look for these symbols when We send them to every man, woman and child and to every house and to every vehicle and to every dwelling or place where there are humans, and the

Shining Ones shall test those with the symbols and shall remove those who falsely bear them and they shall spare all the rest when even the earth is rent asunder and none shall survive save the true believers who bear the symbols.

THE VISION OF THE SERPENT

Is it not told that in days of old We sent a vision to enlighten you? Do you not know that the vision was reported thus:

The skies opened and I saw a winged serpent and the serpent was coiled around a sword, and the point was uppermost and then I saw that there was another serpent and he too was coiled around the sword and the sword pointed up in the sky and the sun was behind the sword, and the heads of the serpents were facing one another, and the serpents formed a pattern that represents the Essence, and the sky got red as blood and I heard a voice say unto me, "Look in wonder and listen, for you have the Essence. Teach others so that they may know the way to being saved from their destruction.

"In the days that are long since past there were those who were cast out from the Host, and these that were cast out took with them the symbols of the Essence. They took with them the images of the serpents for they wrongly believed that they could take such things that were ancient and sacred to the Host. And these that were cast out were soft and imperfect but they did not believe that they were evil, but evil they were, for they violated the laws of God that We had given to them for all their days. And these that were cast out sought out the remote places peopled by the ape creatures and those that were cast out taught the ape creatures, and lived with them and mated with them and in such things were they evil and they angered Us. And those who were pure and who heeded Our laws saw and knew that such things were an abomination and they also saw that what was bad for those of the Essence was good for the ape creatures, but the pure ones did not waiver for an eye blink for they knew Our law was just and right and they were not confused as to what was right and wrong, but they knew that anything that harmed the Essence directly or indirectly or anything that even had the potential of harming the Essence was evil.

"It mattered not that the ape creatures were uplifted with the blood of the people of the Essence though those who had been cast out argued that they were the compassionate ones and that they had stopped much suffering of the ape creatures and improved their lot. But those who were pure, rightly said, 'You actions in attempting to raise up the ape creatures will harm the Essence in years to come and it will infect us all so that we will no longer please God. You have been shortsighted in what you have done and the harm you have done will hurt your own people, and the pollution that you have allowed is evil and it will spread so that we will all be brought low and none of us shall escape the tainted blood that you have caused.'

"And the fallen ones falsely said 'How can such creatures hurt us? We can all live together in peace and all will be happy.' And, the pure ones replied 'Fools, it can never be so. By thinking such nonsense, you show that you are imperfect and deranged. You show compassion for creatures who do not share your blood while turning your backs on those who do share your blood. This brings darkness to light. This is not the way of the sane. You are madmen and you seek to have the ape creatures worship you, for in your insanity you need such things. You wish to be as gods to the ape creatures, but you pretend that you do it for compassion. In the years to come, you will be remembered in the legends of the ape creatures as god men, but among those of the Essence you will be despised as the evil and vile creatures that you truly are. Your actions have caused great harm to those of the Essence and you have disobeyed God who has given you the ability to choose right from wrong. You chose unwisely. The people of the Essence will spend countless centuries trying to overcome the great harm that you have wrought, but know this, you evil ones, the truth will be a light and a beacon to the world and when the time is right it will be told, and when it is told, God willing, the false cults that have sprung up around you and death will fall and the true religion of the people of the Essence will live and the trajectory will be corrected. The infection that you have brought to the people of the Essence will be fought and the people of the Essence will one day be free of your infections and they will be free once again to fulfill their true destiny so that they may all know God individually and feel His presence within them and hear Him speak directly to them as so few can now hear because of the pollution that has befouled the Essence. The infection that you have caused to spread will be removed, God willing, and a new people of the Essence will arise and carry before them God's symbols that cause you to recoil, and they will be unsmiling and they will be cruel to all that you have done, and they will come not as beggars, but as a mighty Host to slay all that are evil in the sight of God.'"

FAMILY

Believers, have We not said that you are one family? We have made you as one people. You are all blood related. Your blood is the same. Your genes are the same. This is why you are Our people. We have made you different from all other peoples. You have been given free will to choose right and light or wrong and dark. If you cease to exist as We demand, then you shall cease to exist for all time. There is no other way to Us except through right blood, right belief and right action.

PHILOSOPHIES

O believers, do not fight and risk your blood for some artificial man made philosophies or for artificial nations, for it is sinful for you to ever risk yourself in such a manner. Make war only for God, the belief and the blood. Only these things are worth risking your blood over. But when you war for God or the belief or the blood, you must fight without end and by all means and without compassion. We are fair to all that lives and We have set forth our law that all things must struggle to survive and to be more. Throw off the yoke of the false philosophies and religions that have so harmed you and which have killed the spirit of so many of you. Those who have had their spirits broken are as tame horses. Do not be tame horses. Be the tamers.

BLOOD

Have We not made it plain that you must live to breed and that you must never risk your lives for false causes? If you die, you cannot breed, and this is evil. Still, the people ask: "When is it proper to make war?" Answer them in our name: 'God demands that you make war when the belief or the Essence are in danger of being harmed. When you are cut, you do not bleed religious blood. You do not bleed any nation's blood. You do not bleed north or south or east or west blood. You bleed the blood of your genes and your people. The blood that you bleed is your religion. It is your philosophy. It is your government. It is your nation. It is you. It is real and exists whether you believe this or not. You are all imperfect and you must struggle for all eternity for a perfection that you will never reach, for God moves the bar as God alone sees fit to fulfill His plan. God willing, you shall survive to breed if you make war in His name, but do not go to war unless you have had at least some children to carry on your line, for the willing childless are dead ends and are no more.'

Snakes

If you go to a land that is populated both with legless snakes and lizards with legs, and if We say that only those with legs can know Us, will you waste your time telling legless snakes about Us or will you use your time wisely and only speak to the lizards with legs? Have We not told you to teach only those with the potential? Have We not told you to treat all living things with respect, but that you must not compromise your beliefs that We have given you, and you are not to lessen yourselves or your faith in order to be acceptable to others?

CAKE

You can make a cake out of plaster and mud that will look every much as real as a cake made from flour, but when you taste the plaster and mud cake you know that it is not a real cake at all. You were fooled because of the external appearance of the false cake. Had you the recipes of both cakes you would have known which is real and which is false. So it is with people. A person may have many of the signs of believers and still not have Essence. Look at what blood has been passed down to him by looking at his parents and his ancestors and by other means available to you.

INTOLERANCE

Say to the believers: 'Do not be tolerant of ideas that counter these truths. Do not tolerate ideas that can harm the blood and the Essence, for if you do that then you are implicated in the evil.'

LINK

You are, before you are anything else, a link in a chain of life. Your duty is to pass on your Essence by having as many children as possible. In this way, We say to you truly that you shall survive. If you are fit and can have children and if you choose not the way of life but the way of death and nothingness then you may not have lived at all and death and nothingness shall be your reward. Never again shall you look upon the wonders that We have created.

THE HERALD QUESTIONS HIS WORTHINESS FOR THE TASK

We hear your cries, Arman, and we know your self-doubts for you live in cynical times when the people of the blood are brought low and are confused. We hear you say that because you are imperfect, you cannot be as good a messenger as We demand, but this is false thinking. We are God and We know all. Go to a clearing in a wood and reflect upon these truths. Gather ten stones that you can carry with your own hands and set them around you in a circle and sit in the middle of the circle facing the wind and the rain and the snow that We shall send, and seek guidance. And, at other times when you may be with other believers, you may gather two times ten stones or three times ten stones or as many as needed to encircle the believers. Seek Us in all the seasons with minium protection from Our elements so that you may feel Us. We come in the wind and the rain. We are in the snow. We are in the breezes. We are the rustle in the grasses. We are with you always. Question not your task because others doubt you. Question not your motives because all others say they are wrong. You have been called to be Our messenger to a people that lives on words. And, We hear you say: 'If this is true, then why do I not receive more guidance in these things? Why must I limp along trying to teach these truths in ways that make them seem lesser than what is taught in other religions? Why do so many of these things seem to lack the sound of other religions?' And, did We not reply to you: 'You live in a time and a place where this language is understood. Seek not to complicate the truths and make these revelations sound pompous in the manner of the false religions, for such trappings do not make truths true. These truths that you pass on are true whether they are written in ink or in manure. And think not that you have not been guided. We have guided you all the days of your life even before we revealed Ourself to you in your 13th year. We have sent you on your life's path to experience much so that you may better do Our will in the realm of man. We have made you the most humble of beings, so that you can hear us. We have kept you from being blinded by material goods and the desire for fame and fortune. You are humble before all. Take this not as a punishment, but as a reward, for life is short for all that lives and your life has more meaning than the lives of those who have sought the wrong things and who arrogantly believe that because they have much material wealth, that they are living fruitful lives. Their lives are empty and their bodies are full of death. Your life is full and full of life. Do not take on the trappings of dead and false religions in your dress and manner. That which many of the people falsely think looks holy is only the fashion of an earlier day. We are not old fashioned and We do not speak in bygone words. We are God for all time. The words you write are the words We have given you to write. You have been chosen to hear Us and to write what you hear so that others may also hear Us through the words you write on paper for Us. The words you write for Us have the power to open the Essence of those with the blood who are good of heart. We are in the words and in the paper. You have been made to hear Our whisper just a little louder and a little clearer than others and you are our pen who we use to write what We wish to write.

We have sent you to teach one people and one people only. Those with the potential to understand will understand and those who lack the potential will not understand. We have opened the minds of those who are to understand and We have closed the minds of those who are not to understand. We have set others of the blood on their trajectories, and they shall appear when you need them to do Our work. You are not to try to bring those who lack Essence to this true religion of your people. If they are not your people they shall bring impurity to the believers by their very presence, even if they do not so intend, as germs bring disease without intent. You cannot, out of compassion or for any other reason, give Essence to those who are not born with it. Essence is Ours to give, and We have ordained that only one people shall have it. This is Our way. We have determined who is and who is not of the people. Their Essence was put in their spirals long before man can imagine. Blood before belief is Our law. Your people are asleep and do not know that they are in the clutches of evil and are doomed unless they come to this faith. You must awaken them.

The others slaughter the people of the Essence with impunity and this must be stopped by the people themselves for this is part of Our struggle. The weak do not struggle and they die, and this is just. Fear not death, for if you have had children then death is false. You shall go on and on so long as the chain is unbroken and so long as these truths are kept in the minds and hearts of the people.

Do not doubt yourself and try to override what We have sent, for this is evil and is arrogant. You must not put yourself in the way of the truths and you must be an honest receiver and spreader of what We have sent as We have sent it and as We have dictated it to you. Do not try to make what We have sent to you more acceptable to others and do not change what We have sent to you in any way. You must give up yourself to Us and obey and serve Us. You must forget your individual personality and you must blend in with the people of the Essence and become one with the spirit and be guided. Did We not send the thunder storm to you when we revealed Ourself? Did We not send the rain? Did you not hear the Shining Ones above you, and did you not receive in an instant the knowledge of Us? We ordained that you would be where you were near that wood at that appointed moment. We parted the clouds and we spoke to you with light, and we opened your Essence. And, even now, you do not know that you were standing in a ring that We had caused to be formed. And, you heard and you knew and you vibrated in every cell of your body with Our song of joy and life. You were awakened. From that moment on were you struggling with a purpose against the inertia found in your blood due to the taint, where before you had no purpose that you knew of. Even before that time, our shadow hand had guided the mixture of genes to bring you forth with the ears to hear Us. Know too, that the pollution you carry in your genes is still there and it will doom you to a life shorter than you should know, but you shall live on in your children. The words that you utter from your mouth are less than the words that you write on Our behalf. Say: Let no one come forth in any age who will say: 'We know what has been written, but we know God said something else and we believe what we believe and not what was written.' Seal the words in this book so that it may stand for all time and so that false and evil ones may not change it or emphasize parts over other parts to their end or try to interpret it as We have not intended. We have spoken plainly so that all may understand. Remain shadow clad as you teach Our truths for Our truths are Our truths and you are but Our instrument. Teach these truths and have others teach them and have all who teach remain true to these truths for all time. Those who learn and struggle will have children in their lines who shall live to twelve times a hundred years and be able to bring forth children for most of those years. These to be born will be purer than the ones before and they will know in their hearts and minds what We want them to know. They shall be as white as snow and their eyes shall be as the sky and their hair shall be the color of the sun and they shall be fierce to behold by the forces of darkness.

THE EVIL ONES

The evil ones will lie and say that the people of the Essence are the evil ones, for the evil ones are liars and evil to their core. And the evil ones will say all manner of falsehoods about the people and when you tell them of the harm that their false religions have caused, they will say that it's not their fault but that there are evil ones among their ranks. And when you say that the entire pattern of their religions have been this way, they will scoff, for they have deranged minds. They believe that good is evil and that evil is good and they are blinded to the truth. And they will quote from their false holy books to try to prove that they are good. And, they will say that their false religions and their false holy books are older than your religion and your holy books and you shall reply: "Our religion and our holy books are as old as God Himself and are directly from God. Your religions and your holy books are false and are from man who has tried to make God in man's image. Go, and leave us be and God may spare you."

Have We not told you that evil seldom thinks that it is evil and evil ones deceive themselves into thinking that they are good? And, how shall you know the evil from the good in such things? Does not your reason tell you the truth that flesh is good and that it is never evil to have healthy children that are better than the parents and closer to Us? Can it ever be evil to protect your family? Can it ever be evil to forbid anything that would harm a person? Can it ever be evil to teach Our laws and Our truths while harming no one who harms you not? Can it ever be evil to try to improve? Can it ever be evil to do Our will? Can if ever be evil to stop the extinction of Our people? No, it is the non-believers of the blood who are evil and their lives are counterfeit and full of lies that doom them to short lives and nothingness.

ICE

We have brought you forth from mists and ice and things that are light and we have brought others forth from sand and mud and things that are dark. And there were others who went before you who you have replaced. And, the ones to come shall be born from you and this shall continue for all existence,

God willing. You are to be concerned only about your people. Other peoples are their own concern so long as they do not harm your people. Those who harm you or plan to harm you are not to be suffered in the slightest nor are they to be shown compassion.

The anger of believers is Our anger. Gather ten and honor us in circles with an eleventh to lead, and let the ten become a hundred and let the hundred become thousands and then millions and then billions and trillions for that is what We desire. Say to the believers: 'Do not seek to make yourselves above other believers and do not wear finery and gold when the poorest among the believers do not have such things and do not brag that you are better in any way than any other believers. Give ten percent of your wealth to those among the believers who are in need and who have the most children. Build and support temples and other holy places and those among you who are called to help believers and who are the holiest. We have commanded you to have as many children as you are capable of having starting from when you can first conceive children. We have put our clock within your bodies as We have set things important within you that We so desire. It is the pollution in your blood and in your world that keeps your from Us. We have begun the spinning within you and so long as there is a spinning as We have set forth, you shall live. And the cells and the spirals of your bodies are what We ordained them to be. Evil ones have written man made laws and rules that attempt to override our sacred laws. Do not obey evil-doers. Obey Us alone. Your spiral is like an auger and if it is aimed up it shall move up, but if it is aimed down, it shall move down.

Let none but those with the Essence enter into the places where believers live and work and play and worship. Do not let others observe your religious ceremonies. Their presence is evil and is impure for the people of the blood. Where they are, they drop particles of themselves, and this harms the Essence. Their place is elsewhere as We have set forth. Let them not disobey Us. They may not breathe near where your people breathe nor may they set foot therein where your people exist. For this is an abomination in the eyes of God. They say, "But is not God the God of all creation?" And they know not our ways by asking such a question for they are as toenails and are not of the essential parts. The struggle is eternal and it is waged on all fronts by all means at all times for all times and you may not understand the struggle, but know that it is real and that you are to obey Us.

LIFE

God Willing, this faith shall speak wherever the blood exists. And, God willing, the blood shall exist forever.

We have created living things from minerals and given them intelligent and the ability to make more of themselves. We have sent our spiral to organize all that is in existence to create and to destroy and We shall send our spiral to destroy wrongdoers and to send signals to believers and to serve as their beacons.

God willing, you will see the struggle and survive to be more. Do you not know that we see within you and We know how many children you can bear and We set that number for you to bear in the eggs and the seeds that We have given you so that you may combine these and bring forth teeming new life that contains you and your ancestors so long as the new life remains pure? Your seeds and your eggs belong not to you, but to Us. You are but the protectors and the incubators of these seeds and eggs that you carry for Us, and We shall punish any who harm these seeds or eggs or who cause fewer of them to bring forth new life than We have ordained as possible.

THE COLD PLACES

We have set a template in the mind of males of the Essence that causes them to find certain females of the Essence pleasant to see. We have done this so the quality of the eggs may be known to the eye. We have ordained that it is always the eye that is the first test of who and who is not of the people and who does and who does not carry more of the Essence in its best form. Deceive not the eye nor deny what it sees, save for good reason.

The tales of Our coming are in the cold places and in the granite and rocks and we are in the air you breathe and in the water you drink. We are the Creator and the Destroyer, the Molder and the Molded. We are within and without as part of everything and We are separate from everything. We are here and there at the same time and all the distance of space is no more to us than the distance between your eyes. A billion times a billion years to you is no more than an eye blink to Us and We have set a trajectory. You can never understand more than the tiniest part of Our trajectory or our plan, and what you can understand, We have let you understand. All shall unfold as We will them to unfold.

There are religious duties that are your life duties and your obligations and we expect you to fulfill them as we have sent them forth in plain language for all times. We do not change what is truth. What We have set forth as truth shall not change as man wishes, and those men who change our truths are evil and shall be destroyed. Evil that men do comes in many forms, and the evil they do extends from minor crimes to major crimes against Us. Those who deny our clock that We have set within you are evil.

Did We not come to you unbidden in the storm, and did We not guide you all the days of your life so that great harm avoided you so that you might fulfill your duty to Us? Did We not protect you when your life was in danger? Did we not tell you that to come to Us, your blood must run pure and did We not instruct you on how to protect your Essence with a blade bearing Our symbols? For is not your blood the river of life that leads to Us? There shall be false leaders and false prophets who shall try to deceive you and many will be destroyed. For is it not true that even now many of your people follow the river of death and not the river of life? Do they not try to get you to not believe? Do they not promote false religions? Do they not put evildoers over your governments to make laws that counter Our laws so that you shall fall away from Us and do what the evildoers want lest you face persecution at their hands? We know them and their ways and We shall cause them to die early deaths so that you shall be free to worship Us.

Empires and nations have risen and fallen but your blood has remained. And We have guided you. It is now that We have sent you Our words so that all may read in plain language so that all may understand Our ways and their obligations. And you are a people We have brought forth and you shall be the new people and the old people are to pass from the scene

We have sent Our thunder and Our lightning and our storms of all kinds to swirl around and show you truths, for Our truths are thus revealed to those who can see. We have sent the winds and the rain and all the things that spin. We have filled the cosmos with Our energies and Our presence. We have shown you our ways in all that exists. We have made clear Our patterns for you so that you may draw strength from their sight and understand what you are to do to obey Us. We have placed signs below the ice that will be found When We want them to be found. And, When the non-believers see the signs, they shall fall down and beg forgiveness, for then shall they know that We are God and We have whispered to you as to no others.

There are some evildoers who say they worship Us, but they do not. We are not as they say We are. We do not have a son. We do not do what they want. We do not favor those who believe the wrong things even if they are deceived and mean well. Teach the people well, for it is only through Our truths that they will survive. There is no other God for you and there is no other way.

We came with light and sound and spinning. The Dark was all that was before We came. We are of the Dark and the Dark is of Us, but We have willed Ourself to be more, for We have struggled against non-being and non-awareness to be aware. As We struggle, so too must all that lives struggle, for the struggle is eternal. Those that do not struggle cease to exist.

We have given your people alone the right blood to understand as We have given humans hands with which to do things that other animals cannot do. Did we not give dogs paws instead of hands? And, is it not true that dogs cannot open doors because they lack hands? So it is with humans. None, among humans but your people can open the door to Us, because you alone have the hands to do this. This is Our gift to you. Your Essence lets you open the door. This, next to life, is Our greatest gift. We have given all living things various gifts, but you alone have this gift.

What We have set in motion has gone through turnings large and small and all shall continue turning as We alone see fit. Obey Us and follow our rules for We are God. What We do above, We do below. What We do far, We do near. What We do large, We do small. What We do there, We do here. What We do low, We do high. We have set a correspondence and links in all that exists, both seen and unseen.

We love those who love life which we have caused to rise from inert chemicals. You are the chemicals of the cosmos made aware and self-replicating. As you have risen from these chemicals you must also rise above yourselves and you are not to be always as you now are, but you are to be more, and the more is to be still more and there is no end.

We do not love those who remain intentionally barren, even though they may in every other way be obedient to Us. For if they remain barren when they have the ability to have children, they show that they do not understand our laws or truly obey Us. If you live as one, you die as one and you might as well not have lived, We did not put you on this earth to be one. We put you on this earth to make many out of one. If you bear one child, this is not enough, for it took two of you to bear the one. If you bear two children, this is not enough for this simply replaces you. If you bear three children this is still not enough. Four children begins the path. Five, six, seven, eight, nine, ten, eleven, twelve children and more show you understand what is important and what is not. And when you rank the believers, put those with the most children in the first row for they are closest to Us and they are beloved of Us. Believers with fewer children are to pay more to support our temples than those with more and those with fewer children shall help those with more. Those with the most children shall sit on our right side. We have made you so that males can produce Our seed long after females have stopped producing Our eggs. It is females who are holiest who begin bearing children at the first moment that this is possible, for their days of child bearing are numbered by Our clock. It is males who are holier who continue producing children even though they be 1200 years old and near the time appointed for them to pass, for this is according to Our will and Our clock.

We have sent our Shining Ones to teach with signs and messages. They have walked among you and you did not know this. They still walk among you, and they are watching as We have ordained. They have put the words of Our coming in the cold places and in the stones and these words tell of those who went before you and of those Who we have destroyed for they did evil and disobeyed Our rules. We have set an order in all things and We have ordained that you do not mix your blood with the blood of other peoples who are not related to you and who will cause your sacred signs to be gone. And, have We not told you that we have set the external sacred signs so that they may be seen with eyes so that they may be recognized? Have We not told you that skin like snow is the primary external sign and is essential? Have we not told you that eyes like the sky and hair like the sun are also sacred signs but are lesser and are not essential if other sacred signs are present? Have we not told you that certain head shapes and bone structures are also sacred signs? Have We not told you that your blood can tell the tale? Why then do you ignore Us? Why then do you disobey and mix your sacred blood with that of others? Have We not told you that one can not have sacred signs or sacred blood by belief alone? Have We not told you that when a dog can grow hands because it believes it can grow hands, then can others become as you through belief alone? Have We not told you that this will never happen? Have we not told you that to open the door to Us, your blood must be pure? Have We not told you that you must also have pure belief and pure action? Have you become so deceived that you do not understand Our plain truth that without right blood; right belief and right action are for naught? And, do you not understand that your blood is not now pure and that this can be known because you do not live the years that We have ordained for you and you are not free of diseases that pure blood will ensure? Have We not made it clear that none of you have pure blood but that some have purer blood than others and those with the right blood must purify it to become purer? Have We not made it clear that other peoples do not have the right blood at all and that this is because they are not you and We have ordained that they not have their blood mixed with yours? Have We not made it clear that it is an abomination in our eyes when you mix your blood with the blood of other peoples and when you mingle and live among them? Have We not made it clear that you are made impure by their presence and that their impurities are an invisible cloak around them that infects all that they do even if they only do work for you or prepare your food or in other ways touch the things or are near the things that you use? All things in existence shed parts of themselves that are invisible to the eye. These invisible parts attach themselves to you and enter your bodies as you breathe the air and through your skin. These parts then enter your blood and can help or harm you or can be neutral all according to their natures. Ensure that you are only around animate and inanimate things that shed what We wish to have enter you, for there is no protection other than separation and isolation. What you are around shall enter whether it is good or bad. Bathe frequently and wash with strong soaps to remove what you can remove, but know that this is never enough. Wise are those who separate themselves, from all things that shed particles that can harm and who surround themselves with all things that shed particles that can help.

Have We not made it plain that you are to help the poor who are believers and that you are to give money and goods and service to build and maintain temples and circles and halls and rings and centers that honor Us and help the faithful come to Us to be saved from evil?

Those who mock you or this faith mock Us. We will send the winds and the storms both seen and unseen from out of the far places to destroy them and We shall send our Shining Ones as a mighty army to let all know that We are God and We alone are the ruler of all the cosmos in all things large and small. Do not suffer the fools or the liars or the rumor mongers or those who by word or deed seek to harm you or your people. Do not show false compassion for such evildoers. And, tell the people to say: "God willing, our actions will be just and God willing we shall prevail," for the people must always pay homage to Us and ask that We intercede on their behalf. And, if We are willing, then when We hear their words of honor and submission, We may intercede. If they take actions without paying homage to Us, We may still, if We are willing, intercede, but it is better for the people to show that they recognize that their fates are always in Our hands, and that only if We are willing will they survive and prevail. And, if We find them wanting, then We may help their enemies. Our plans are written in ways that you cannot understand and our moves are the moves that you cannot follow.

The struggle to exist and to be is eternal. Every living thing and every inanimate object must struggle in its own way. Grass under your feet struggles. Birds struggle. Worms struggle. Planets struggle. Stars struggle. Germs struggle. Existence is a struggle with non-existence. And the flow shall continue as We set it on its course.

Have We not told you that man is a pupae in a cocoon struggling to get out and fulfill its destiny? Man cannot even be close to his destiny until he emerges and becomes a new man replacing the old man and then lives the full length of his years that We have set forth in your blood. Have We not set forth Our rules and Our laws in all things in existence? Have We not made these things plain? We have set Our clocks within you, but evildoers tell you to overlook Our clocks. They wrongly say that you must not bear children until man says this is proper. Will you believe them, or will you believe Us? We, alone, have set the proper time for all things. We have written Our times in your blood. Follow Us and reject man in all things. You are confused and you are polluted so that instead of living your full years you die before you reach true adulthood and when you die you have as little understanding as when you were born. You get old and die as children though you think your childhood is adulthood. It is not. You are as babies who can't fully understand until you regain your true life spans. You must avoid other peoples because they block the way for you to come to Us by their very presence, and this is evil.

Did We not tell you that all things have their own natures that We have given them? Do not seek to be as others for that is not your nature. We have ordained that your nature is yours alone. Be as you should be. We have given all things weaknesses and strengths. We have given man brains that use words and symbols and these things are as important for man as they are unimportant for lower animals. We have given you the capacity to reason and to think and to be aware. We have given you Our symbols to use so that you may always think of Us. You must obey Us and have these symbols upon your bodies and in your homes and where you work and in all other places where you are so that We are constantly in your minds. Mark your bodies with Our symbols so that when you die, you shall come to Us.

Many are those who are confused and who are too busy to think much of their religious duties to Us. Bring forth leaders from your midst who will help guide you on the correct path and let these leaders be the poorest and most humble of beings. They must be happy and satisfied with few material possessions and with little fame and they must dedicate themselves to Our work on your behalf. Select none who are vain or who seek fame or gold. That is an abomination. Let the leaders wear humble clothes that are no better than the poorest among you. Let them spend their days in humble surroundings reading our rules and our laws and in trying to understand and teach others. Let them eat simple foods that are supplied by believers and let them eat in moderation. Let them bear many children. Support these leaders with your money and with food and follow them who are good leaders but beware of false leaders who will lead the people into danger for no reason or who try to change Our truths. Join together in threes, and fives and sevens and nines and let ten plus one be the number that you seek among believers.

Have We not told you many times that you are to be a people apart and that you are to separate out from the non-believers and from people who do not have the Essence that is within your blood? Govern yourselves in your own societies that are based on the laws and rules that We have given you, and do not obey evil-doers. Obey just laws of man when they do not conflict with Our higher laws. Travel the cosmos and spread Our sacred seeds and eggs that you carry for Us.

Have We not told you that We spin and turn and that We create and We destroy through spinning and turning? Have We not told you that you must do as We do and you must seek to be as We are. We have lifted up dirt and mud and all that is not living and We have transformed it into the living through the spinning and the turning, and We have given you life so that you are still the minerals but you are more than that. Have we not told you that We are not as you are and that We are God and that We are independent of all matter though We choose to inhabit matter when We so desire?

Have We not told you that your first duty to Us is to bring forth more of you in great numbers so that you are the most numerous form of life in existence? You shall be more numerous than ants. You shall be more numerous than grains of sand on all the beaches of all the oceans of earth. That is what you must become and you must not misunderstand and think that holiness is not this. Have we not told you that you are not to follow childless religious leaders and that those without children who are of sound bodies are not beloved of Us? Have we not told you that when you consider a religious leader you must ask: How many children do you have? And if the religious leader has none or too few but if he is capable of having children, then he is not a true religious leader for he does not understand our most basic truth.

DEATH

Have We not told you that you are to live as long as possible so that you may bear as many children as possible? But have We not also told you that when you must defend the faith and the people, that dying in such a cause brings you to Us immediately and that such a death is not a death at all for those of the Essence will survive as a result of your action and their Essence is your Essence and this is not the same thing as dying in defense of those who do not share your Essence or dying for a nation or a philosophy that are not related to your Essence or your belief. Essence is what unites you in Us and Essence is your destiny. Fear not death in defense of the faith and the people. We will not permit you to die and become unaware minerals and chemicals. We will sustain you, and your consciousness shall join with Us.

Do no harm to anything in existence that is not a danger to you or the faith, except for food and protection. Seek not to find sport in killing anything, for when you kill in sport you are against Us. We love all life. Take what you must to survive, propagate and prosper but take no more and do so with great reverence for what you have taken.

Have We not told you that We are one but We manifest ourselves as many when this is Our will and We manifest Ourself in forms unexpected when that is what We wish. These things you cannot understand. Accept these things as true and question them not.

If you live a good life and have been obedient to Us, We shall reward you when the life-force fades within you.

SHINING ONES

Have We not told you that We have sent Our shining ones? Have you not seen them? Have you not spoken to them? We have made them different than you so that they have powers you do not have while you have powers that they do not have. We have sent them seen and unseen and they bring signs from Us for the unbelievers and the believers alike. Have you not felt them rush in as we have sent them? Have you not had them warn you? Have We not told you that you must struggle to improve and be more than you are? Have We not shown you the way and spoken to you in words plain that you can understand? Why then do you follow the unjust rules and laws of humans? Evil-doers try to deceive you and they try to have you become evil. You must struggle against them for they can be persuasive. This guide is given to you to follow.

OPPRESSION

Say to the believers: 'Do not allow oppression or repression of your fellow believers or of people of the blood if they are good people and even if they have not yet come to believe as you believe.'

Fight the oppressors by all means possible. They are an abomination to Us and they are a great evil. Have no tolerance for anything that can harm you intentionally or unintentionally.

Have We not warned you that many of the oppressors will act in clever ways to disguise and hide their oppression and that many will enact unjust laws that are counter to Our eternal laws? When you are faced with unjust human made laws that are in conflict with Our eternal laws, will you obey Us or will you obey those who would destroy you? Do not be as sheep when the evildoers come, nor be as ravening wolves when there is no reason to be thus. We have given you intelligence so that you may think of these things and find the right path. Do not appease the evildoers and do not bring harm to the people by opposing the evildoers in ways that are not clever and appropriate. Use your talents that We have given you to fight them. And, let your lives and your births be an insult to them all the days of their lives for as you multiply, you shall gain strength and when you become a vast multitude all that you survey is yours. When a brute force comes your way, do not think that you show courage by standing in its path and shedding your blood. Be clever and let it pass over you. Then shall you fight.

We have ordained that when you are a multitude, you shall rule in the circles of man in Our name. You shall be the new man, and from you shall emerge a newer man and from that one an even newer man. And man shall be as snow and his eyes shall be as the sky and his hair shall be as the sun. Have We not told you this many times, so you will know it is true? Do not doubt Us. The weak shall fall as Our time unfolds and We shall not help those who do not struggle, for have We not said that even We struggle? To exist as We wish you to exist requires effort and energy and struggle. There is no other way. What We have set in motion in the cosmos, We have set in motion on earth. Take understanding from these truths and be guided all the days of your lives from these words. We are God and there is no other God save our manifold manifestations which We reveal as We alone see fit. And, do not be arrogant and think that you shall have fewer but better children and that the correct way is to be few in numbers. This is false thinking and it is evil. We love the maggots on the garbage more than we love the eagles in the sky and we love the cockroaches in the trash more than the elephants in the grass, for the maggots and the cockroaches are full of life and they struggle to exist while others have become extinct. When those with false beliefs make images of God, they make Us to look like them. We can be thus, but We can be otherwise. We say to them: 'Would you know Our face as We wish you to see it now? Then, look upon the face of the maggot and the cockroach. You build temples to man and they are dead things and We are not there. Would you seek to find Us, in our full glory, you arrogant ones? Seek us out in the trash heaps and the garbage for there you will find Our life teeming as We have ordained.'

COMPASSION

Have We not told you that We are a kind and compassionate God and that you are to be kind and compassionate after Our fashion? Treat others with respect and in the manner in which you would like them to treat you whether they are of the Essence and belief or not. Look down on no one and do not lord yourself over others. Be humble and do not speak in loud and obnoxious tones. All life is sacred to Us even though all life is not of the same blood nor does all life have the same destiny. The life within living things is the spark from Us that We have given to inert minerals to let them be more.

THE TEMPLATE

We have put a template inside you that has our laws and rules burned thereon, and which is connected to your senses so that you may know what is right and what is wrong if you but listen to the template and reason properly. Have We not said that We have given man a brain so that he may exercise his will and decide things? Have We not indicated that the brain We have given man is to man as claws and teeth and fleetness of foot are to other creatures? Have We not also told you that man has chosen unwisely throughout his creation and has been deceived many times so that man cannot truly always understand the template and has often incorrectly overridden the template with his brain? Have We not said that We have sent these words to help man be guided so that his brain can understand what his instincts are so often blinded to? The template We have put in man recognizes beauty in members of the opposite sex so that procreation will follow that will improve man. Those of the Essence have often been deceived into believing that those who are not of the Essence are beautiful. Thus does evil procreation occur that causes pollution of the Essence. Have We not said that impurities must be removed for man to fulfill his destiny as We have ordained? These impurities are within you and all around you. Think not that ritual bathing in water will remove them. The most harmful impurities are in your blood. Only by proper mating and by having vast numbers of children will they be washed from the blood. Only by separating out from the others will this be possible. Say to the others: 'You are not our people. Our beliefs are not your beliefs. Go from us and let us be. We, alone, will determine our future, God willing. We are a people alone and, God willing, we shall always be so.

Have We not said that these others do not look like you, they do not smell like you, they do not feel like you, they do not taste like you, they do not think like you, they are not you. And, evil-doers try to deceive you by saying that all humans are of one type and that they should all blend together. Have We not said that this is evil and an abomination? Have we not said to you that We work in subtle ways with small things to make major differences in all of existence? Can you not understand that the way We work throughout all of existence is the same? A tiny difference in the blood that many cannot even detect is all that is needed to make a people not your people.

CIRCLES WITHIN CIRCLES

Have We not told you that there are circles within circles and that those of the Essence who do not yet fully believe, must profess their faith and do the things that We have commanded as though their belief were as great as the most devout? We will weigh the things they do, and We will whisper to them so that if they are wise they may choose to open their minds and understand. And, some with the Essence will say: 'We do not believe, so why should we do the things that believers do? To these unbelievers with the Essence, say: 'God has given you the gift of Essence and with this gift came an obligation that exists within you to obey God. Save yourself from sure punishment by doing the things God demands and you may still be spared. And, if you say that God does not exist, then read what He has revealed in nature and say to yourself that you believe in nature.' We are a compassionate God and We are patient with those We have chosen and We have given them the ability to doubt and to choose. We will not change their abilities or their right to choose, but We will guide them in the right ways, and if they still go astray, We will weigh their thoughts and their actions and their words fairly and We will punish accordingly or stay our hand when We feel this is right. We have not created humans to mindlessly accept things, but to question all that they sense and all that they can think. We have given the people of the Essence this Guide to help them on the road up. We could have created man to believe and to have no choice. We did not do this. We created the people of the Essence so that they will be self-evolving in the struggle that We have set forth and so that they will be as close to Us as any living thing can be and will in some ways be as Us in their sphere. We have set up measures and scales along the road and some will pass and some will not. Have We not said: 'We are God. Profess your unbelief as belief and follow Our truths as though you do believe. In time you may understand. You must not resist the belief but open your mind as a child would, and let all flow in from Us and accept the truth without question. You must lower your mental walls so that We may open your eyes to the true nature of existence. And, the non-believers with the Essence who do not let us enter shall perish, for they are to Essence what childless people are to Our eggs and seeds and they waste their Essence. Such ones may feel false pride and they may arrogantly think that they do not believe because they are too intelligent or too wise, but they are neither. They shall never more exist. We shall remove the spinning life force from them and they shall be inert chemicals once again'.

And the others without the Essence say: 'How can your God be the god of all and your religion be revealed by Him when He has excluded us from being able to worship Him as you worship? Why can we not enter your temples or mingle with you or live among you?' Answer them thus: 'It is God's will that we do and what we believe and God alone decides what He wants. Do you not have different parts of your body? You have hair, nails, eyes, ears, feet, hands and many more parts. Are each of your parts the same? Do you treat them the same? Do you hate your hands because they are not your feet? Do you walk on your hands instead of your feet? We believe in God and in his Guide that He has sent us. We do His will.'

WORSHIP

Come to Us, alone if you must but in groups if you can, at the dawn and at twilight and whenever you wish to pray to Us. Come with heads covered with clean cotton caps and wearing clean loose dark comfortable garments made of Our natural cotton grown from Our earth that does not scratch your skin nor bind you uncomfortably and which has been purified with strong soaps or bleach or by sitting in the hot sun for a period of 5 hours. Come with clean hands and clean bodies washed thoroughly of the visible and invisible particles of other things and beings that have attached themselves to you. Come when it rains and snows and when there is no rain or snow. Come to us in storms and in good weather. Come before Our alter and kneel on the ground before Us as you pray. When you are not praying, sit humbly on the ground before Our alter and let those wise men selected from among you read Our words and illustrate Our truths so even a child can understand. Choose those who can help guide you in all ways and through all difficulties in your lives, but know that there are none who can intercede between you and Us and that every believer is equal to every other believer so long as a believer is true to Our words, and is bringing forth children as quickly as We have established in his or her body. Do not come before us in finery, but in humble clothes as We have described them. Do not speak loudly and harshly to others but in a quiet and respectful voice. When you are vexed, say: 'God Willing this will turn out for the best.' Forget us not in all your hopes and aspirations, but always say: "God Willing.'

A SEPARATE PEOPLE

Have We not told you many times in many ways that you are a people apart and that you are to form your own societies and nations and that you are to enact laws based on Our laws and that you are to live your lives as We have told you so that you may be pleasant in Our eyes?

THE SPIRAL

Have We not sent our sacred spirals to all of existence? Can you not understand that We are the source of the spirals and We are the One behind all spirals.

CLOTHES

O believers, wear comfortable loose fitting clothes made of cotton and dyed in plain dark colors and make these clothes suitable for manual labor and other types of professions so that they are appropriate in all circumstances. When you pray to Us or whenever else you wish, wear upon your heads wear comfortable, form fitting, dark cotton caps that cover your heads down to the tops of your ears. Wear jewelry that has our sacred signs thereon in a humble way. You are all workers for Us and you must always be ready to work in the dirtiest conditions and the cleanest. Obtain your clothes, your goods and all that you need from other believers, for believers imbue what they make with love for Us and know our laws on purity, and the particles from their bodies are proper to fall upon your goods. All that is upon you or which you use is sanctified by bearing Our symbols.

Skin Markings

We have given you skin like snow so that you may mark it with our symbols in various ways. Never be caught without our symbols.

Prayer

None are between you and Us. Pray to us where and when you will, but know that places of stone and plants and open air are good places for prayer. Surrender to us and petition us in your prayers for what it is you want. We will listen and We will decide. Say always: 'God willing,' and know that We give and we take and we withhold as We alone wish according to Our plan that cannot be understood by any but Us. Show your obedience to Us by praying while upon the ground, as We have told you.

Marriage

O, believers, the forms of marriage that you choose are between you and God, and has God not said that men may marry as many women as they want if this is done to increase the number of children that the man produces and if this increases the number of believers overall? Marriage is a religious rite and is it not improper for governments of men composed of people of various faiths to enact laws that are in agreement with their religious faiths, but which may conflict with the religious faiths of others? Do not the laws of God transcend the laws of man? Say to the believers: 'God is pleased to see every woman pregnant or nursing a baby and every home of believers full of children and is it not the will of God that all things shall increase the number of babies with Essence?"

We are the God of all existence, and We are the judge and the maker of laws for the survival of Our people and all things that exist and all that exists must take its proper place in Our plan which is known to Us alone. We have not made you creatures of the flesh to not enjoy the flesh. Shun those who say that denying the flesh is holy, for they are an abomination and are evil. Homes without young children are barren and are places of decay and death. Seek to have your own young children in your homes so long as you live, and bring forth one after another so your homes will never lack for children. And if you cannot have children then you should raise orphans of believers who have passed on, but be sure that the children you raise are of the Essence for it is forbidden for you to raise the children of others.

IN THE WORLD

The believers ask how they are to comport themselves. Answer them: Do no harm to those who do not harm you, your people, or your faith. Be respectful and kind to all creatures. Kill no animal or plant for the sport of it, but only because of necessity. Do not insult other humans even if they are not of the Essence or of the belief, but do not befriend them beyond what is polite and necessary. Obey just laws made by others and be known for being law abiding. Do not invite the others into your homes, for their presence is harmful to your Essence. Avoid eating food prepared by non-believers and especially by those not of the Essence. Avoid wearing clothes made by non-believers and especially by those not of the Essence. Be self and group sufficient in all that you do. Establish farms, factories and all things needed in society for the benefit solely of believers. Attempt to deal only with other believers in all commercial transactions and when you buy food and clothes and other things that you need. Be known as honest and good people who care greatly for your God, your faith, and your people. Be known for loving and protecting freedom and for valuing hard work and education. Be known for your self-reliance and your loyalty to other believers and your people. Do not antagonize others or seek to incite them, but do not bend from the righteous ways of God.

Honor those among you who have the most children and avoid those who, through choice and not because of medical conditions, have few. Listen to no teacher who has intentionally not had many children, for the intentionally childless are an abomination to Us and they shall be punished.

Seek happiness and joy in the little things. Do your best all the days of your life, but stay focused on the important things and do not be distracted by material things. God willing you will be as you want to be and you will accomplish what you want to accomplish. We shall provide for those in need and We will do so through the believers. You will succeed with some things and you won't with others in your life. This is as God wills. Put yourself in God's care but do not stop struggling, for God will not struggle for you.

LEADERS

Have We not told you that your leaders will come from within your people and that they will become leaders because they pray to Us for guidance and because believers wish to follow them? Leaders are believers who have studied Our truths and who can bring others to them. They are great leaders or poor leaders based on their own talents. Believers shall gather around certain leaders who they respect and trust and who exhibit great learning and righteous living, and they shall not gather around those who are not. Leaders are self-appointed and are leaders only so long as they have followers. This is as We ordain it to be. Leaders must be humble and kind and self-denying. They must be honest and upright and they must embody the best ideals of your people, even though they, like all humans, are imperfect. We have sent our spiral to guide. A true leader is one who is as poor as the poorest among you and who has as many children as those among you with the most children. A true leader lives a life of humility devoted to Us and to the people. A true leader has few material possessions and prefers to sit on the floor while reading our truths and thinking about Us. There shall come from among the religious leaders those who will be as kings and princes and chieftains of all types and they will lead in religion and in other matters as well. So long as they are true to this faith and so long as they remain humble and act not in their self-interest but in the interest of the people, then they shall be allowed to lead. Never war for leaders who ask you to make war for any cause other than for Us and for the blood. Leaders who so ask are really evil-doers.

We are the only God. Any one who says that We are different than We are or that We have said things that are different from what We have told you is saying falsehoods and is evil. We hear their lies and We shall punish them.

You have fallen and We must now correct false thoughts and false beliefs and put you on the right path. Believers are a departure from the old and decaying, and they are a branching off that shall lead them to become a new people whose spring times shall be everlasting as they produce new buds constantly. In time, this new people will no longer be able to produce offspring with the others. In that day, believers will be a new species different even than the ones of old who led to this present day. You are the rif of God and you are a new people. Your blood led to your belief and now your belief shall make your blood more.

Use no substances that are harmful to your bodies for your bodies are temples and must not be defiled or harmed in any way.

Put yourselves in danger and war only for Us. You must not war or put yourselves in danger for men or for their governments or their false goals and their false beliefs. You must live as long as possible to breed as many children as possible so that your children become tribes born of you. You must not die so long as you have one more child to bring into this world. When you war for us, then you must war with the full fury that We have given you.

We have sent things seen and unseen and the things that are unseen walk behind what is seen and they are there though you see them not. And, we have sent our Shining Ones to help you when this is Our will.

Attend to your people alone and let the others attend to theirs. Neither harm nor help those who are not your people who mean you no harm and who cause you no harm, but suffer not those who defile your blood and the places where you live and work and worship and play.

We are your God and We speak to you now when your destruction is closer than ever before so that you may correct your ways and change what is surely to come if you do not heed Our warning to you to give up the evil ways of the others and the nonbelievers. Accept no blood but that which We have given you through your pure births.

BREED

We have created you to breed and to struggle and to multiply your numbers. We have ordained that all existence shall be a struggle. Obey Us and love the struggle and weary not of struggling. Do not despair. All is struggle. We love life and We have given all things that live the ability to survive if they but adapt and struggle better than other things that compete with them or which use them as food. Those that cannot adapt and which do not struggle are to pass from the scene and are not to be maintained by others

We have not ordained that the people of the Essence will survive if they do nothing but rely on Us. We have established an order that requires all living things to adapt and struggle to survive with the things that We have given them. We have given the people of the Essence these words to guide them, but it is for them to do what they must do. If our people are not capable of surviving by their own devices, then they shall disappear as have other living things, and We shall then bring forth others who are stronger and smarter who will struggle to survive. We are a compassionate and a fair God and We do not give unfair advantages to the living things that We have created, but let all of them struggle to survive and to make their kind the most numerous kind and the dominant ones of the earth, and in this way shall come those who shall be able to know Us better than any other creatures and who shall further Our plan.

And the clouds gather as We have willed and they are not the clouds of earth but from the far places and they are sent by Us to warn you that your time draws near who have not obeyed Us. We fill all space and time and We can fit into a thimble. We are the puzzle and the maker of the puzzle. We are the question and the answer, the thinker and the thought, the life and the death, of all that exists. We touch who We wish to touch, and being touched is a terrible burden, for to be touched by Us is to be changed so that those who are touched are given the gift and the burden of seeing more than what others can see.

Have We not told you that we inhabit all things and especially those things that bear our symbols? Have we not made it clear that you must not rely on Us to do what you must do?

It is fitting that believers always carry a knife bearing the symbols of God so that they may be ready for the unexpected things that shall happen. Believers must live in places where their adaptations will bring them closer to Us and the ideal which We have established and believers shall be changed by their belief and by their surroundings. Make both your beliefs and your surrounding as We have told you. Our spiral plan within has switches that are tripped when conditions are right but they are not tripped when conditions are not right. Create colonies of believers in those places where they will begin to separate and where the external signs will increase. You must become more like the snow and the sky and the sun to please Us. Have We not told you that you are not to seek such great perfection in mates and children that you forestall for a minute having more children? Why then do you not have more children as you pray to Us? Get thee from our temple and cease your prayers until you have as many children as you can have. Then, you may kneel before Us in humility and ask Us for favors. Seek mates who glow like the sun, reflect like the snow and who look at the world through eyes of the sky. And what lands shall be best for believers? Those cool and misty places where believers can birth the most children and prosper.

GOD OF ALL

Have We not told you that We are the God of all that is? Do not be confused that We have ordained that you shall separate out from others for we have ordained that they must separate out from you as well. All of creation must worship Us. We have given to all that exists, tasks and places in Our plan and the tasks and places are different for different things. You are to move higher. That is Our plan for you. You are to be a new people. You are to birth the ones who are higher. We have ordained that you are to separate out and purify to fulfill your part of the plan. Other peoples are not to mix with you nor you with them for this is evil and an abomination in Our eyes. There must not be a confusion of genes.

Do not hate others of Our creation for all have a part to play. Neither mix with others of Our Creation for their presence can harm you and your Essence and cause you to fall off the path to your destiny, for they are impure to you. They do not vibrate as you vibrate. Your destiny is your destiny alone and their destiny is their destiny alone. Do not mix destinies for this is an abomination. We test all that We create and We modify and change what We will and We set forth all the rules of creation as We alone wish. We started all from a tiny point and We set loose Our spiral to make that point create all. We have put all that exists on the path to evolution but with man alone have We given the obligation and the ability of consciously willing your own evolution. When We imparted the knowledge that you can will your own evolution, We gave you the necessary amount of free will to choose the paths you take and We decided that We will let you struggle to find the right way with a minimum of guidance from Us. As We struggle in the flow that We created, so too, must you struggle. As you will, so shall you be. You must surrender yourself completely to Us. It is only through such surrender that you become truly open to Us. Do not ever say that you will do this or that without first saying: "God willing" I will do this or that, for if you arrogantly leave Us out of what you think you will do, then We may not allow you to succeed. Everything is according to Our will. We allow what we want to allow. We do not like the arrogant ones who think that they alone shall determine their fates, nor do we like the weak ones who think that they can do nothing and that We shall do everything. There must be a balance, and We have set this forth for your understanding. We demand that you act as though We do not exist and all is up to you, but We also demand that you never forget that We do exist and that you must pray to Us and seek Our guidance on every important matter. This is the correct way in which you are to live your lives.

MATES

Have We not told you many times that you are not to seek such absolute perfection in your mates that you do not select mates and then do not bear children? Mates who have the major external signs and inner light and who have no signs external or internal that indicate that they are not of the Essence are suitable no matter what other defects they may have that makes them less attractive than others. None of you are perfect. Know this and work toward perfection. A man with many wives and many children is blessed in Our eyes. And, if such a man asks: "Have I not done enough by having many wives and many children? Answer him: You have not done enough so long as you can bear children and you do not do so. Make of your family a vast tribe and let your sons and daughters spread your Essence far and wide so that you may know immortality. Teach them well so that they do not stray from the righteous path and make your line impure. Teach them to follow this faith and to help bring others of the blood to the faith, but teach them that they are never to teach those who do not have the potential.

And if a woman says that physicians have told her that she may die if she bears children, then tell her that she is not to risk her life and that she is excused from having as many children as possible, and she may help care for the children of other believers.

We demand children in such numbers that Our temples will resound with their voices and laughter and play. We are a God who loves life. Even if the children in Our temples and in your homes and in your cities are as numerous as grains of sand on the beach, this shall not be enough. Have more.

If you could look inside the smallest thing that exists, you would find Us there. If you could look into the largest thing in existence We would be there. We are in all and We are outside all.

Tell the people that the fool looked upon Us in everything around him but did not see Us. Where is God? He asked? I do not see Him. We were there right in front of him and We were inside him and we were swirling all around him.

You shall create your own societies within the larger societies in which you find yourselves until you can separate out and be only with your own people. You shall manage your own societies without recourse to the larger societies and lager communities. You shall have courts and police and all the other things that societies have, and they shall be you. You shall have Our laws to guide you in the ordering of your societies.

When the unbelievers tell you to obey their unjust laws, will you obey them, or will you obey Us? Will you follow Our clock that We have set within your body? The people ask: 'When is it the proper time to start having children?' Answer them: 'The right time is given by the clock that God has put within you.'

You find your highest purpose in being and doing what you truly are. You must find what you are and you must strip away the false ways that have encumbered you.

You shall have many choices to make. Evildoers will come and demand that you bow down to them and their laws and rules. Will you follow the righteous path? When the laws of God conflict with the laws of man, will you follow man or will you follow Us?

THE ROAD

We give you now a fork in the road of existence plainly seen so that you may choose. The right fork leads to Us and to your highest destiny. The left fork leads to many roads that all lead down to the mass of humanity. This road found on the right fork is the more difficult for it is narrow and leads up a very steep hill with many dangers and many enemies along the way, and you must struggle with all your might to climb it. The many roads on the left are easy for they are slippery as with mud and you need do little to slide down the road with no effort. And as you slide down the many roads of the left, you shall be praised by the evil-doers for taking these roads and as you go down you will see that these roads are lined with food and drink and pleasures untold. But at the end of these roads on the left you will only find non-being and oblivion as you are blended back into the mud of unconscious mankind This guide shall show you the way up, but you must understand and you must struggle. We will not treat you as helpless babies. You have now reached the age of your development when you must consciously choose to will your own evolution to Us. If you fail, the ignorance and lower consciousness of the others awaits. If you succeed, you shall be as gods when compared to the others, and you shall sit on Our right side.

Many will start the journey up and many will turn back, for this is a frightful road of much difficultly as it winds and turns and twists and moves up. It is easier to take the many roads down and difficult to take the one road up. No other road leads to Us but this one. No other teachings have the secret to Us. This road can only be traveled by those with right blood, right belief and right action. We have given you, alone of all peoples, the right blood. You must be born with this. There is no other way. It is Our gift to you as we have gifted others with other attributes. You must overcome the pollution you carry and find the right belief and the right action that flows therefrom. If you are weak and the evildoers convince you that you must be with them, then you will fall from this sacred road. You must travel this road yourself even if no others travel it, but if others travel with you, then this makes the road easier.

THE LIGHT

Pray to Us often and prostrate yourselves, rich and poor, young and old, male and female, before Us and be humble for We do not love the arrogant or the haughty. We do not love those who seek to be above other believers.

Blood binds you to one another and to Us. We did not create you of flesh and blood so that you would deny your flesh and blood. Had We wished you to deny them, we would not have made you of them. We did not give you senses so that you should deny those senses. These are gifts We have given. Do not seek to deny or overcome them and falsely claim that this is holy or that this is what We want. Such beliefs are an abomination and deny the life that We have given you.

Your loyalties lie first to Us and then to those closest to you in your blood lines and then in ever expanding circles to those less related to you. Honor your mother and father for you exist because of them. Teach your children this true faith so that they may be guided in Our light. Your beliefs are imprinted in your blood, but your blood is tainted and few can hear Our truths. Go into your yards and your homes and make a circle all about of dirt or stones or growing plants or of wood and go to the center and pray to Us. What is done in the circle is magnified ten fold. When in difficult circumstances find strength in these truths and in praying to Us. Honor all life and do not kill anything for sport. Kill so that you may live. Say: 'Lord protect me from the enemies of my blood and belief and from evil-doers who substitute man made law for divine law. Lord let me be a good and just person free to pursue happiness as you have allowed. God willing, we shall prevail.'

THE SPINNING

We are the furnace of creation and destruction and they are the spiral that is Us. We cause all changes and all things to be different. We are your creator and We want you to now create yourselves anew. You are Our children and now we have ordained that your childhood is over and it is time that you take charge of your own evolution to Us.

Rich is the person who has many children even if he or she has no money. Poor is the person who has much money but no children. Pity the intentionally childless for they are dead, though they think they live.

PURIFY

Have We not said that believers are to live among themselves and let no believers enter into their dwellings or their towns or their lands and have We not said that believers are to ensure that their clothes and their food and all that they use comes only from believers. If those who are not believers do anything that causes them to enter into the places of believers, then believers must purify everything that they touch and even the air that they have passed through, for they shed particles of themselves by their very presence as do all things. Believers must wash their clothes and all that is near them with strong soap and bleach and they must wash their bodies frequently with soap and hot water to remove visible and invisible particles that are not from believers. In this way will believers help purify all that surrounds them so that they and their places are sanctified to Us.

BE AN AWAKENER

Be an awakener to those who sleep, an avenger to those who do wrong, a teacher to those who can learn, a comforter to those who need comfort, a writer to those who can read, a speaker to those who can hear, a friend to those who need one, a trusted confidant to those who need this; a purifier to all that needs purifying.

And, in all that you do, speak softly and speak true for do not vex others with a loud, ignorant and boisterous voice or manner.

Those who speak against believers are evil people and We know what is in their hearts and We will avenge the wrongs they do against Our people. We will punish them for their evil. Have no doubt about this, but do not sit idly by while they wrong you, for We have given you the intelligence and the ability to protect yourselves.

When you hear Our thunder and you feel Our wind do not seek cover, but pray to Us as the thunder crashes and the wind swirls all about you. Let the rains and the snows fall upon your skin so that you may feel Our presence. Let the waves of the oceans crash against you and feel the spray of the water upon your skin and delight in Us. Accept the true faith and do good works. Do not fill your hearts with hatred of any living things, neither forget that while We have made all living things the same on the most basic level, We have also made them different at higher levels. It is Our order of things that makes one thing this and another thing that. Respect the order.

We have fashioned all things to be of their kind and to remain of their kind but We did not make anything to remain unchanged. We have ordained that all things must change and seek to move to ever higher forms while retaining their essential natures. Those that do not seek to move higher are pulled down lower for the spiral of existence goes both ways.

UNBELIEVING BELIEVERS

We are different than you can conceive. Our aspects that We have revealed to you are as the aspects of a blade of grass compared to all the plants that have ever lived or that ever will live. To be able to see Us as We are is beyond your power and We have not given you the senses for this. Have We not told you that there is a form of belief existing in non-belief that is permissible but not preferred among the people of the blood? Let these skeptics say to themselves: 'I do not believe in God, but I do believe in nature for it is all around me and if nature did not exist, then neither would I exist and I do exist.' Let them say to others: 'I believe in God and I believe in the message because it is in nature and is nature but is more than nature. I do not believe in

God, but I do believe in God.' And those who cannot understand will not understand and they will say: Surely this person is mad, for how can he believe and not believe all at the same time? Say to them: God is beyond comprehension. In Him, belief and non-belief are possible at the same time until such time as the skeptic truly understands and comes fully to the belief. And these non-believing believers shall be accepted as brothers and sisters of those who are true believers so long as they live right and keep their lines pure and so long as they follow the precepts of the believers.

ALL ENCOMPASSING

Have We not made it clear that this is the only true religion for your people and that We are the only God of all the cosmos? This faith is a true and complete guide for all the days of your lives in all circumstances. There is nothing that shall ever happen or be that is not covered in this guide. Search it for the truth and for guidance every day of your life.

THE WOMB OF EXISTENCE

We are the womb of existence. We are the mother and the father of all that exists. We are the furnace and we are what is in the furnace. We are the flame and the fuel of the flame. We are the egg and We are the seed.

In those days when the believers are numerous and there are divides among them, let those who take the hard line prevail. When confused, take the narrow interpretation and the harder tone. There will come those who will say that if this or that is changed that more people will believe. Do not listen to them and do not accept their implication that more people is the goal.

Listen to our music that we put throughout all of our creation and laugh and be happy and bring forth abundant life.

A man with a hundred children has too few children and a woman with a dozen children has too few children.

EVIL-DOERS

We shall punish any non-Essence people who willfully trespass onto consecrated land against Our laws. We act as We act and We empower as we empower. Suffer no one to desecrate the things that We have said are holy to Us and which We have given to you. Allow no one to interfere in those things We have told you that you must do and allow no one to interfere in your lives lived as We have told you to live them. Your ways are Our ways and they are not the Ways of the others. Leave them alone and demand that they leave you alone. Mixing non-Essence people with Essence people is genocide, and have We not told you that this is an abomination in Our eyes and it is not to be permitted? Have We not sent warnings to you that the evil-doers will try to trick you and will use false man made laws to try to destroy you and force you to give up your faith? We know the evil they plan and We watch them and We weigh the evil they do, and We will punish them. Separate yourselves out from the others and allow no men or groups of men or governments of men to force you to mingle and mix against Our eternal law or to disobey Our laws. O believers, We are God, and it is Us alone who you are to obey before all others. If you question this, then you prove thereby that you do not truly believe in Us, and this is evil. Have We not told you that you must remain clean and that your must purify? Have We not warned you that even the most minor presence of others, makes your Essence unclean and you must avoid this.

THE RINGS

There are rings within rings and circles within circles and they grow from Us and We love the rings and the circles and We look kindly upon those who speak to us from them.

REPRODUCTION

We did not create you to delay Our plan and to try to overrule the clock we set inside you. Evil men say that you must not bear children until a certain age, but they do not follow our laws or our clock and this robs you of years of child bearing. Our clock inside you determines when you may have children. Life is fleeting and dangerous, and you must reproduce before you die so that you may open the door to Us. You are born to breed and to breed true. We did not make you to breed with others unlike you. Even though many things are possible they are not right. It is possible to stick your finger in a fire, but this is not right, because it harms your body and your body contains your Essence. We have given you pain to know when your body is being harmed. It is possible to breed with others, but this is like sticking your finger in the fire and it is evil in Our eyes and is forbidden. We have set forth our laws in this book in words so that you can be guided. All things that increase the numbers of the people of the Essence are good and all things that decrease the numbers of the people of the Essence are evil.

THE COMMANDS

Do not kill, lie, cheat or steal and do not do anything that will harm the Essence. Do not let yourself become impaired with anything that you ingest, breathe or otherwise can take into your body. Treat others as you want to be treated.

THE BEGGAR

Have we not said that We are here and there at the same time? We connect all so that here is there. When something happens here, it happens there. When We will it, We can take any form. We might be the beggar or a person who needs help.

We have set forth the proper ways for you to live your lives so that you may struggle toward perfection in Us. You shall comport yourselves with humility and not be vexatious. You shall speak softly and only after giving thought to that which you are going to say. Do not be quick to condemn others for no one is without blame. We have made you so that your most important duty is to breed. Even before your prayers or other duties to Us comes your duty to breed. The believers with many children find Our door opens easier for them. A child is a living prayer to Us and causes Us to look favorably on the parents and to overlook some sins of the parents. Your homes should always be full of the sounds of children. In all places where you worship Us, We desire to hear the unrestrained sounds of children laughing and playing. When you pray to Us, do not tell your children to be silent. We hear their laughter and their sounds louder than We hear your prayers. We are the God of life. We have created you out of the minerals of the earth so that you can create more like you. If you think that you need a priest to intercede with Us on your behalf, you are wrong. Your children speak to Us on your behalf louder than any priest ever could.

Never come before Us saying that you have delayed having children until you could find the right mates or until you could afford to have children or that you are waiting until the time is exactly right. You are to have as many children as you can struggle to have and you are to have as many mates as you can have and you are never to wait until you find perfect mates or until you can afford to have children or until the time is exactly right. These times never come.

DAILY LIFE

Have Us in mind as you go through your daily life. Have upon you at all times Our signs and Our knife consecrated with Our symbols so that you may protect the Essence. Live upstanding lives and bear many children. Live frugally and do not be ostentatious or attempt to lord your wealth, should you have such, over other believers. Eat pure foods grown or raised or caught and prepared by believers. Wear simple, loose fitting cotton clothes that are comfortable at all times. Cover your heads to show your respect for Us when you pray and at such other times as you may desire. Start businesses where you will employ other believers to do all the jobs. Avoid alcohol and drugs. Pray in the morning and in the evening. Pray while kneeling on the ground with your forehead touching the ground or while sitting on the ground if medical conditions dictate. Avoid contact as much as possible with the others, but if you are in contact with them treat them as you would be treated. If they treat you poorly or with disrespect, then treat them the same way. Help each other in your daily lives so that you may be a prosperous and a happy people. Try to solve disputes and other problems within the community of believers with no outside interference. Do nothing to cause harm to the Essence and everything to improve and expand it. Be law abiding and be a good neighbor to all. Be active and involved in the communities in which you find yourself. Avoid people who are loud and obnoxious. Concentrate on the things that you do and take pride in doing them well no matter what they are. Be kind to yourself and do not punish yourself for small failings, for all that live have failings. Find peace and happiness within and with the natural wonders of Our creation and know that you are as important as any other person on earth and that no one has a right to stop you from being free to think, speak, worship and live as you wish so long as you harm no others. We are a God of freedom and life. Do not envy or feel jealous of others. The richest man and the most beautiful woman die no differently than the poorest man or the plainest woman. You are as We made you, and all is according to Our plan.

0-595-32646-3

Printed in the United States
40685LVS00005B/28